HEART OF A THIEF

AN UNFORGIVABLE ROMANCE, BOOK 1

ELLA MILES

CONTENTS

Free Books

Want to read along for **free** as I write a new novel—*Not Sorry*?

Want to get my **free** bonus novella—*Aligned: Ever After?*

Want to know when I put my books on sale for **free or 99 cents?**

You can get all of the above and more goodies here:
EllaMiles.com/freebooks

WARNING!

I'm the villain in most romances.

I'm a thief that steals happily ever afters.

Except unlike most romances, love doesn't conquer me, I conquer it.

I've stolen countless women from unsuspecting men.

Gotten my one night with them.

And then watched the heartbreak that occurs in my wake.

Love doesn't survive once I enter the picture, if it ever existed at all.

Although, stealing Sloane might be my greatest challenge of all.

Asher is a villain trying to a put a horrible life behind him by doing the only two things he knows to do: surf and steal. Sloane is an angel that runs a charity helping children needing a fresh start. Asher will do anything to have her. There is just one problem...she's about to marry another man.

WARNING: *Heart of a Thief* is a standalone steamy, contemporary romance series. There will be more books in the

I grab a beer out of the mini fridge while I wait to see if Danielle is coming up or not. I pop the cap off against the counter in my hotel room and then bring the cold liquid to my lips as I stare at the door.

I met Danielle three weeks ago. It was a lucky happenstance really. Well, lucky for me, not so lucky for her. I met her like I meet most of my targets—in a bar. She was with her fiancé, minding her own business, just having a drink at the bar, when he was called away for work. That was when I stepped in and gave her the attention that she was so desperate for.

That's all it took. One night of being nice to her, and I knew I could steal her from her fiancé. I knew it wouldn't take long. I probably could have had her that night if I really wanted. But that's not my game. Cheating isn't enough. Many a men take back fiancées or wives who have cheated on them. No, I don't entice the women so that they will cheat on their husbands. I hit on the women to steal them and make them mine—at least, until I get bored with them.

I'm not looking for anything long-term. I've never dated a woman for longer than a few weeks after claiming her as mine. Others, I get bored with much faster. I'm not really after the women. I'm after the chase that comes with stealing them away, and that satisfies the rush I used to get when I stole objects instead of people.

I don't know which makes me a worse person. Stealing things like cars, money, or jewelry. Or stealing women and their hearts. But, this way, at least I don't have to worry about going to jail.

I sit on the edge of the bed as I take another sip of my beer. I thought tonight was the night I would claim her. I thought tonight was the night I would steal her away. But, as every second passes, I become less sure of myself.

Maybe Danielle loves her fiancé, Wade, more than I thought she did.

I hear a soft knock on my door. Once, twice, and then a pause before the third knock. I grin before I down the rest of my beer and toss it into the trash can as I walk to the door. I open it and widen my eyes when I see Danielle standing outside my door, like I'm surprised that she is standing here even though I'm not the least bit surprised.

"What are you doing here, Danielle? Shouldn't you be in bed, dreaming about that fiancé you are going to marry tomorrow?" I ask.

I haven't stolen her yet. Not fully. I don't win until she's broken up with him, and I've had her in my bed.

Danielle wraps her arms across her chest, covering her cleavage that was sticking out from beneath her sparkly white dress that she wore to the rehearsal tonight.

I didn't have to do much to get Danielle here. At least, not tonight. All I did was show up at the rehearsal. I made an appearance in the background, and it was enough to convince Danielle that she might be making a huge mistake.

"I'm not getting married tomorrow," Danielle says.

"Oh," I say, my voice dripping with sadness that isn't the least bit real. "Would you like to come in?"

She nods, and I hold the door open for her. She walks over to the edge of my bed and sits down. I walk over to the mini fridge and pull two beers out. I open the caps on both and then hand one to her. She takes it, loosely holding it in her hand. She stares at it for a while, not able to look at me.

I keep my distance until she is ready to talk. Leaning against the counter next to the mini fridge, I sip on my beer.

"I broke up with Wade tonight," Danielle finally says.

"I gathered that. Why though?"

She looks up at me with puppy-dog eyes. "Because I don't love Wade anymore. I love you."

I look at her seriously and say, "I want you."

She hears *I love you* though. It's clear from the goofy smile and blushed cheeks.

But that's the one thing I won't ever do. I won't lie to these women. I can't help it if they hear what they want to hear.

I put my beer down and walk over to her until I'm standing between her legs. I take the beer out of her hand and place it on the counter. Her eyes follow me.

I push her back on the bed, and then I take the off the T-shirt I'm wearing... She bites her lip as she stares at my abs that have formed from surfing every day.

"Tell me you want me to fuck you," I say.

Danielle sits up and unzips the back of her dress, letting it fall to her waist, revealing her white lacy bra that holds her perky breasts in, away from me.

"Fuck me, Asher."

I grin as I grab ahold of her dress and roughly pull it off her body. She lets out a gasp.

She grabs at my neck, trying to pull me in so that she can kiss me. I let her pull me into her. I let her kiss me, and then I turn the kiss into rough kisses that show her what I really want.

"You like it rough," she says.

"Don't you?" I ask.

"I like anything with you."

I flip her over on the bed, and she lets out another surprised gasp.

I slap her ass. "I'm going to fuck this later, but first, I have to claim your pussy."

"God, just fuck me already. I can't wait," she cries into the pillow that she is now face down on.

I sigh. "They never have patience," I mutter to myself, annoyed that I can't take my time to properly enjoy her body.

"What?" she asks.

"Nothing," I say, hitting her hard on the ass, causing her to cry out.

I shove my shorts and briefs down and pull out a condom from the nightstand. I quickly slip it on before she finds a way to get herself off without me.

"Ready?" I ask, pulling her panties down and positioning myself at her entrance.

"Just fuck me already."

I do. I push inside her tight pussy that I know is anything but ready for me. I've barely spent any time turning her on, but if this is what she wants, I won't object.

She moans loudly and then quickly starts screaming, "Yes... yes," over and over.

I keep thrusting until I come, not concerned at all if she comes or not. I'm an asshole after all. Although most have called me worse than that.

She must have come because she screams loudly, followed by nothing.

I pull out of her and go to the bathroom to clean myself off. When I'm done, I stay in the bathroom with my hands clenching either side of the sink as I look at myself in the mirror. I can't handle this woman much longer. It was hard enough to pretend to like her to get her to want me, but now that I've had her once, I don't think I can keep up the act to fuck her more than that. I'm ready for the implosion to happen.

I walk back out and dig through my suitcase to find a fresh pair of briefs to put on. After I do, I glance over at Danielle, who is now under the covers of the bed. Her cheeks are flushed, her brown eyes heavy, and her long brown hair is a mess on top of her head.

"That was amazing," she says.

I nod and force my lips to curl up into something that resembles a smile.

"I'm ready to go again if you are. Or if you want to sleep some first..."

I take a deep breath, ready to tell her that I'm through with her, that she can't stay here, when I hear a loud pounding at my door.

I hold up a finger and then walk to the door in just my briefs, not caring who is on the other side. I throw the door open, and before I can register who is standing there, a fist flies at my face and hits me square in the nose. My body jolts backward with the hit, and I put my hands up to my nose as another hit rains down on my face, followed by another. My nose is pouring blood now, and I'm sure it's broken. My eyesight is blurry, but I think I make Wade out through the haze. Or, at least, my prior experiences with ex-fiancés verify that he is most likely on the other end of the fist that keeps coming at my face.

"Wade, stop!" Danielle screams, running to my aide.

I hear Wade breathing heavily.

"I'm done. I'm done with both of you. You're a rotten scumbag who deserves to be locked up in prison. And you're a lying, cheating slut. I'm done with both of you."

The blurriness finally leaves my eyes long enough for me to see Wade stumbling out of my room, clearly drunk. It's a wonder he was even able to aim for my face. The door slams shut, and then I see Danielle standing naked in front of me.

"I'm sorry about Wade. He's just upset that I broke off the wedding, that I no longer love him. He'll get over it."

I walk into the bathroom without saying a word and see that I was right about my nose. It's most definitely broken as blood pours down my face. I grab one of the towels and hold it up to my nose to try and stop the bleeding, but I know it is going to take a while to stop.

"Here," Danielle says, holding up a bag of ice.

I take the bag from her and hold it up to my face.

"It stings," I say, wanting to pull it away from my face.

She laughs. "It will help with the swelling and stop the bleeding."

I keep it on my face and walk back to the bedroom. Danielle follows me.

"I think you should go," I say.

"What? Why?"

"I don't want to worry about Wade coming back and beating me up."

"He won't."

"And I don't think you and I are going to work out. You're not worth my trouble."

Danielle's jaw drops. "I broke up with Wade for you though. I called off my wedding tomorrow for you. I want to be with you. I'll do whatever it takes."

"You made a mistake then. You should have stayed with Wade, or you should find someone else. I'm not the man for you, Danielle."

"He's not going to take me back now," she says, her voice shaking.

I smirk. "No, I don't think he will take you back."

"You fucking bastard! You asshole!" Danielle shouts, raising her hand to no doubt slap or punch me.

At least, this time, I'm ready for the attack. I grab her wrist midair, stopping her from hitting me.

"You are an evil, vile person," she says through tears.

I nod. "I am."

She jerks her hand out of my grasp. "Why would you do this?"

I open my mouth to speak, and she holds a hand up to stop me.

"Never mind. I don't want to know. I don't want to spend another second listening to this crap." She grabs her crumpled dress from the floor and quickly puts it back on, not bothering with her underwear. She cries the whole time.

Occasionally, the women recover after this. They are able to convince their fiancés to take them back. But I don't think Danielle will. And I'm not sure she is strong enough to fully recover from it either.

She hesitates a second, like she is trying to decide if she should say anything or if I'm going to. When I don't, she storms out the door without another word.

I take a deep breath as I go over to the bed and lie down, ensuring the ice pack is still on my face.

Shit, I curse to myself when the ice stings my face again.

If I'm going to keep this up, I need to be better prepared. I can't keep getting hit like this. Next time, I might get a concussion, and then I won't be able to surf. I won't let that happen. Next time, I'll be ready for a hit.

Maybe I should take some boxing classes or something.

I grin. Despite the pain I'm feeling now, I'll sleep like a baby for the first time in weeks. I stole her heart and then tore it to pieces. It feels good.

TWO

Asher

One Year Later

I see the towering wave in front of me. It's huge and getting bigger by the second. It doesn't stop me. Instead, I push my board to move faster as I surf into the wave. My heart pounds fast and hard in my chest as the wave surrounds me, forming a tunnel that can collapse at any second. If it does, I'm going to have to fight like hell to get back to the surface to be able to breathe. I've been crushed by waves like this before and ended up with a couple of cracked ribs that hurt like a bitch and take forever to heal.

I'm not going to let that happen to me again. But remembering that pain doesn't stop me from attacking this wave either. Most wouldn't bother. Not when it isn't a competition. Not when I don't have anyone out here to rescue me if things take a turn for the worse. It's just me and the wave. That's how I like it.

I love the thrill. I love knowing that one wrong move could fuck everything up, even my life. I could die if I don't do everything perfectly.

This is what I live for though. I don't live to win competitions even though I win a lot and the money is nice. I live for this feeling right now—the feeling that, at any point, the ocean could steal my life from me or I could conquer it and live for another day. There is no other feeling like it in the world.

I surf the wave and come out the other end of the tunnel, unscathed. I win—for now. I step off the board and let the cool, salty water refresh me before I begin heading back to the beach. It's starting to get dark, and as much as I would love to stay out here all night, I'm hungry, and I have other cravings I need to satisfy.

Because I lied when I said that there was no feeling like surfing a wave that could destroy you. There is one feeling that is better—the feeling of stealing someone's happily ever after. The thrill of chasing a woman already claimed by another man just does something to me that nothing else can. It twists my soul and makes me want more of the drug that pulses through my veins every time I finally make the woman mine instead of his. It's a drug that pulls me in over and over again, a thrill I can't resist.

But why would I want to?

I'm a thief and a surfer. Both things keep me completely satisfied. And neither makes me feel guilty. I don't feel bad for the women or the men I hurt. I'm doing them a favor really. They believe in true love and happily ever after. They believe in the fairy tales they have been fed their whole lives. I just teach them how wrong they really are. In the real world, love doesn't exist.

"That was some wave, Asher," Luca, my only friend in the world, says.

"What are you doing here? I thought you were supposed to be home, resting, after your concussion. Or are you finally taking my advice over the doctor's and getting your ass back out here?" I ask with a grin before walking over to where my towel is slung over the back of my pickup truck. I toss my surfboard in the back before I take the towel and begin drying my shoulder-length dark hair.

Luca laughs. "Nope, just wanted to see if you wanted to grab a drink and a bite with me."

I stop drying myself off and grab a T-shirt to throw on. "Is that new girlfriend of yours coming?"

Luca frowns. "Hell no. She's back on the mainland, visiting her family. But, even if she wasn't, I wouldn't let you anywhere near her."

I walk to the driver's side of my truck and open the door. Luca is already climbing into the passenger seat without waiting for me to say that I want to hang out tonight. He already knows my answer is yes.

"Why not? I should meet her if you guys are getting serious, shouldn't I?"

I climb in and start up my truck, waiting for the purr of the engine before it fully starts. It doesn't start up right away. I get out and give the hood a love tap with my fist before I jump back in and turn the key over again to get it to start.

"You should really get a new truck, Asher. This thing is a piece of junk, and you can afford a lot better."

I narrow my eyes at him. "Why would I want anything better? The truck still runs, and all I use it for is to get me from my place to the beach. Why would I want to get a new truck? It would be a waste of money. After one drive, it would be full of sand and look just as bad as this old thing. How would I know if the new truck could handle the sand as well as this old thing anyway?"

Luca nods to the truck. "This old thing can barely handle the sand. They do make trucks designed specifically for handling sand and rough terrain nowadays, you know?"

"When this one dies, I'll think about it."

I don't have to tell him the real reason I don't have nice things. People would assume I stole the new car instead of buying it. I've learned it's actually better to live without the finer things in life.

I reach my hand out the window as I drive back to my house —if you can call my place a house. It's more like a shack on the beach. But it has the most amazing view. I love feeling the warm, salty air as I drive the couple of miles back. Luca does the same. You can't help but do that here.

"So, back to your girlfriend," I say.

Luca frowns and grabs ahold of the frame of the truck as we bounce along the dirt road that leads back to my house. "You don't get to meet her—ever."

"What? What about if you decide to marry this one? You've been with her for, what? A month? That's a new record for you. She might be the one. I need to vet her first. And I'll have to meet her at your wedding anyway when I'm your best man."

Luca shakes his head. "Not happening. You are never going to meet her. You don't even get to know her name. You don't even get to meet her at my wedding or even after we get married."

"You do know, it's not possible to hide her from me forever? Hawaii is a small island. I will figure out who she is."

"Not if we move far away."

I chuckle. "Not going to happen, dude. Once here, no one moves away from Hawaii. They move *to* Hawaii."

Luca shakes his head. He's not going to tell me right now. And I don't blame him for not telling me. He knows that I have been looking for a bigger challenge, a harder chase. Most of the girls around here have been too easy to steal from their unsuspecting fiancés or husbands. That's the nice thing about living in Hawaii though. Everyone comes here to get married. So, I always have an endless supply of women to hit on and steal. But, lately, it's been too easy and the damage I have done has been minimal at best. If Luca really is in love with his girlfriend like I think he is, if he can see himself proposing to her in the future, then they could be my biggest challenge yet.

But I need to make sure they are really in love first, that they want to get married. Then, I can plan my move. So, for now, I'll wait. I'll wait for my best friend to fall in love, and then I'll destroy him. It might destroy our relationship, but I doubt it. Most of the men blame their cheating girlfriends, not the guy their girlfriends fell in love with. Well, on second thought, they do blame me, but after a good square punch to my jaw, their anger at me usually dissipates. Occasionally, it lasts a bit longer, but then I've never been friends with any of the men whose girlfriends I have stolen. Luca might hate me after this, but it is a chance I'm willing to take.

I park the truck outside my shack of a house and climb out. "Give me two minutes, and I'll be ready to head out," I shout to Luca.

I run up to the door of my house. Luca doesn't answer me, but I hear my truck door slam behind me, indicating that he climbed out of the truck. I push my unlocked door open; I never bother locking it. There isn't anything in here that is worth stealing anyway. I don't even own a TV. The most expensive items I have are my surfboards. Nobody wants to steal mine when they have their own. And, even if they did, my sponsors would just supply new ones.

That's the key to life—not having anything worth stealing. That's why I don't own anything worthwhile. That's why I don't fall in love.

I walk toward the back of my shack. It's just one room with a fridge and small stove that I rarely use for cooking, a bed, and a dresser. I don't even have a bathroom inside. I have an outdoor shower and toilet. But it satisfies all my needs and ensures that any woman who gets close to me isn't going to stick around for long. No woman wants to live in a shack on the beach, no matter how beautiful the sunsets are.

I reach my dresser and pull out a fresh pair of swim trunks and a new T-shirt. I only own one pair of clothing that isn't swim trunks, and I'm not going to bother wearing it tonight. I prefer to live my life in swim trunks. For one, women find them sexy as hell. They know right off that I'm a surfer without me having to say a word, which makes my job easier. Two, they are way comfier than any other clothing around. And, three, I never know when I'm going to want to go for a swim or go surfing. It's better to always be prepared.

I grab the fresh clothes and lay them on my bed before stripping and heading out into my shower. I rinse the salt water out of my brown hair that is far too long before drying off and heading back in to put on compression shorts, my new trunks, and T-shirt.

I walk outside and see Luca standing with his hands in his pockets, staring out at the sea.

I know he's still nervous about getting back out there again. He took quite a hit the last time he was out there. It was a life-changing, almost life-ending, event. I know he still doesn't know what he's going to do now. He was never the best surfer out there. I've always been better. Always gotten more sponsors. Won more championships. I'm not bragging; it's just the truth.

But a surfer doesn't know how to do anything else. He doesn't know how to live a different life. I know his comment about wanting to move somewhere else to keep his girlfriend away from me was just as much about him. If he stays here and decides he can't surf anymore, he is going to have to face his decision every day for the rest of his life. If he moves where there isn't an ocean staring back at him everywhere he goes, then maybe he can move on.

I get it. I just don't know how he could ever give this life up, no matter how dangerous it is. Life isn't worth living if you aren't doing what you love.

"Ready to go?" I ask.

Luca nods and turns toward me, and then he laughs. "Why did you even bother changing if you were just going to put trunks back on?"

I shrug. "At least they are clean."

"It's no wonder that you don't have a girlfriend."

I grin. He's right about that. I don't have a girlfriend or a fiancée or a wife. I never have and never will. The swim trunks help ensure that. I'm a fling that women think they can fall in love with, but when they realize they can't change me, they move on and deal with the heartbreak they caused when they left the men who actually loved them. While I get freedom. And that's how I like it.

THREE

Asher

"You're going to give yourself a heart attack with the way you eat, man," Luca says, staring down in disbelief, as I scarf down my second double cheeseburger.

I shrug and then shove a couple of fries into my mouth. "At least I'll go out doing what I love and not eating that healthy crap you eat."

"It's called fish and vegetables. You should try it sometime. You might actually find that you like it, and you will feel better when you're working out and surfing."

"Nah, I'm good." I drink down my beer. "So, when do you think you and that girlfriend of yours are going to be moving to the mainland? I need to know when I need to get a new wingman."

"I'm not talking about her. I already told you that."

I sigh. I'm frustrated and bored. And it's been weeks since the last woman. Tara was it? Sara? Cara? I can't remember.

"Fine, then help me pick out my next prey," I say.

Luca laughs. "Not going to happen, bro."

I frown. "You used to help me."

"That was when I was evil and didn't have a heart, like you. I've since grown up."

I shake my head. "You haven't grown up one bit. Just help me find someone who is an actual challenge this time. Sara wasn't enough of a challenge. I was able to get her to sleep with me and break up with her fiancé in less than a week. It was pathetic really."

"First of all, her name was Nicole, not Sara. And, second, you really need to stop. If you don't, you are going to fuck up someone's life so bad that it is going to rebound and hurt you, too."

I laugh. "Not likely."

Luca shakes his head as he drinks his beer. He reclines in his chair, lifting the front two legs off the ground. "Don't say I didn't warn you. It's going to happen. One of these times, a woman is going to hurt you as bad as you hurt them, and I'm going to be there, laughing in your face while eating popcorn. It's going to happen, bro. It's called Karma."

I take a swig of my beer and then grin. "I would love for a woman to try and hurt me as badly as I hurt them. I would love to see one try because it's impossible. I don't have a heart for them to destroy. Remember? I'm the devil."

"You've got that right. But even devils can get hurt. And I can't wait for it to happen to you."

"Whatever. It's not going to happen."

"Because you've been so right about everything before." Luca snickers.

I frown. "I'm right about this," I say sternly, challenging Luca to question me again.

He doesn't. Instead, a slow smile forms on his face, but he doesn't say anything. He doesn't say that I'm completely wrong about this even though I know I'm not. He doesn't say I'm as wrong about this as I was about encouraging him to go surfing with me the day of the accident that almost killed him. He should rub that shit in my face forever. Blame me for his accident. He doesn't though. He doesn't blame me. He has always said that it was just an accident. Completely unpreventable. That it was fate. I don't believe in fate. I believe in taking the world into your own hands and making yourself happy because no one else is ever going to.

"Look, a bachelorette party. Isn't that right up your alley?" Luca says.

I grin and turn in the direction that Luca is looking. About ten women are all scantily dressed in skirts and tight dresses. Glitter and stickers cover most of their bodies along with sashes saying what their role in the wedding is, like *Bride's Main Bitch* or *Bride's Bitch*. They don't understand how easy they make it for a guy like me.

I scan the group of women until I lock in on my target. The bride. She's easy to spot because she is the only one wearing white. She has a sash that says *Sexiest Bride-to-Be* and a crown that has a veil coming off of it.

She's a blonde, which makes me feel torn. I haven't had a blonde in a while, but then again, they are often the easiest to steal. But I'm ready for a challenge, not an easy lay. To my surprise though, she seems like a local girl. You can always tell by the tan or lack thereof or sunburn. She is nicely tanned, obviously used to the strong summer sun here. At least half of her bridesmaids are a weird shade of orange from the tanner they have been using. The other half are burned to a crisp.

The bride though is gorgeous. Her white dress shows the perfect amount of cleavage and is short enough to make her legs look long and toned. Legs that I desperately want wrapped around my body. And, if I play my cards right, that could happen by the end of the night. She doesn't look that in love. She looks like she is desperate for a way out of the situation she is in.

I watch as the group makes their way over to a corner of the bar where the bartender pulls together three couches for them to all sit on around a couple of low tables. The bride-to-be, of course, is given a couch all to herself since this is her special day, when it's supposed to be all about her.

She doesn't know how lucky she is. Today isn't going to be her special day. Today is going to be her lucky day.

"Definitely. I knew you'd still make a good wingman even if you gave up your old ways. You'll always be a monster to me."

Luca frowns. "Just don't forget to leave cash to pay for your half of the bill. I'm not paying for all the shit you ordered. I'm unemployed, remember?"

I roll my eyes. "Stop being dramatic. You weren't going to do another competition for another month anyway. You have exactly the same amount of money you would have had whether you had the accident or not. But"—I pull out my wallet and throw enough money down to cover both of our meals—"since you pointed out my next target and are going to help me convince them that we are cool guys and to not have us thrown out on our asses, I'll pay your bill."

"Not going to happen, bro."

I grin. "Are you sticking around to watch or going home?"

"I'll stick around until you start taking your shirt off, and then I'm out of here. But I'm still betting those women are going to get you thrown out of here."

I roll my eyes. "Always the pessimist." I pick up my beer and head over to the women, putting Luca out of my head.

"Hello, ladies. You all look beautiful tonight. Can I—"

"No, you can't join us," the bride-to-be says.

"Even if I buy you all a round or two of drinks and find the hottest guy in town to strip for you?"

I grin slyly and watch everyone's eyes soaking me in. Even if the bride doesn't want me to stay, her bridesmaids do. They *need* me to stay. Because, unlike the bride, they don't feel special tonight. And they all think I'm the guy who will make tonight a little easier by making them forget that they aren't the ones getting married and most likely aren't even close to getting married.

"Yes!" one of the bridesmaids sitting next to the bride says, taking her life in her own hands instead of waiting for the bride-to-be to answer.

She just doesn't know that I'm not here to have a one-night stand with one of the hot bridesmaids. Although I might regret that because several of the bridesmaids are easily in the top ten hottest women I have ever seen. One is wearing such a short dress that I can already glimpse her perfectly shaved and pierced pussy from where I'm standing.

I force my eyes to turn away from the piercing that I desperately want to see in action. I'm not really sure how it could make sex any better, but I'm sure that it could.

When I look back to the bride-to-be, she is glaring at me.

"So, when's the wedding?" I ask the bride-to-be.

"Sloane is getting married next month," the same loud-mouthed bridesmaid from earlier answers.

I grin. It's a perfect timetable. I don't have a competition for about five weeks. I can seduce this woman, make her fall for me, and get it out of my system before I have to get serious when competition season starts next month.

"What can I get y'all to drink?" Paige asks. She's the bar's new waitress from Georgia, and she has that Southern accent to go with her adorably naive smile.

The women start shouting out drink and shot orders. But I'm not really interested in what any of them are ordering. I'm interested in what Sloane wants to order.

Paige looks to Sloane, and Sloane leans back in her chair.

"I'll have a whiskey." She pulls something out of her purse. "Do you mind if I smoke this in here?"

I know the bar has a no-smoking policy, just like every other bar in the city.

"I won't tell," Paige says, winking.

I raise one eyebrow at Paige. I'm surprised by both women—Paige, for having the guts to say that Sloane can smoke in here when she can't, and Sloane, for holding a cigar in her hand.

Paige leaves to go get everyone's drinks while I take a seat next to Sloane.

"Have you ever smoked a cigar before?" I ask.

I doubt that she has. Someone must have bought her a cigar to celebrate her engagement. That's all this is.

Sloane laughs. "Why? Are you going to show me how to smoke a cigar?" Her voice teases me, but her eyes travel up and down my body, drinking me in.

She might be laughing now, but I'll have the last laugh.

"No. I'm just don't want you spending your night coughing and sick after one inhale. I don't want you to miss the show I'm going to put on later," I say with a wink.

She lights the cigar, takes one puff, and then slowly releases the smoke from her mouth. My eyes fixate on her mouth because it is the goddamn sexiest thing I have ever seen.

"First of all, you don't inhale a cigar. You would know that if you had ever smoked a cigar before. And, two, thinking that I have never smoked a cigar because I'm a woman is the most sexist thing I've heard in a while. And I run my own company, so I hear sexist things all the time. And, three, I would rather spend my evening in the restroom, puking my guts out, than watch whatever show you will be putting on."

I grin the whole time as I stare intently at Sloane's mouth, waiting for more of the sexy smoke to escape her lips. I love how fierce and take-no-crap she is. Women like this are always the hardest to crack, always the hardest challenge. But it will only be a challenge if she is really in love with her fiancé. If she just sees her arrangement with him as a business deal, which I imagine is how she looks at much of life, then it won't be that difficult to get her to cheat on her fiancé. It won't be that difficult to convince her that she could fall in love with me.

"So, did your fiancé get you into smoking cigars?"

She frowns and then puffs on the cigar again before slowly letting the smoke out. "No, I got him into it."

I smile because I don't believe her. There is no way a beautiful woman like her would take up such a nasty habit without a man convincing her to try it. At least, I've never met a woman yet that would smoke a cigar because she wanted to and not to impress a man.

"So, when did you start smoking cigars?" I ask as I casually put my arm around the back of the couch and behind her back. I'm not touching her, but I can tell it makes her uncomfortable because she leans slightly forward.

"College."

I smile. "What brand did you smoke that first time?"

She frowns. "Why do you care what brand I smoked?"

I shrug. "Maybe I want to take it up, and I want to know what brand I should start with."

"Alec Bradley Prensado."

"Who were you with when you smoked?"

"Jessie, Wes, Kirsty..."

I turn to the loudmouthed bridesmaid who has been eavesdropping on our conversation. "Who is the lucky guy that is marrying our Sloane here?"

"Wes Finnigan."

I smile. "So, Wes was there the night you smoked your first cigar, but he wasn't the one who convinced you to try your first cigar?"

Sloane's cheeks turn a nice shade of pink, but I don't think her cheeks are pink due to embarrassment. No, it seems like anger is the cause.

"Fine, Wes was the one who got me started smoking cigars. You happy now?"

"Not particularly." I lean in so that I can whisper into her ear without her nosy bridesmaids hearing me. "I won't be happy until I have you in my bed. And it's going to happen, Sloane. Whether that's tonight or a month from now. You need to have one last fling before you marry the wrong guy or preferably kick him to the curb and replace him with me."

I stand up before she can get a slap or punch in. I've said a very similar line to too many women before. Sloane is the kind of women who will slap first and ask questions later. She's tough, strong. And probably too uptight for her own good. But I'm not sure how in love with Wes she really is. I'll have to wait and see if this is going to be too easy or one of the hardest steals of my life.

Paige is back with the drinks, and I help her pass them out before letting her know to put all the drinks on my tab. When I hand Sloane her whiskey, she is fuming so much that I'm afraid she is going to throw the drink in my face.

She doesn't, but I can tell that it crosses her mind.

"So, who's ready to see the hottest man on this island strip for you?" I ask.

I am answered by an array of hoots and hollers.

I grin and then pull out my phone to start up some music. I start dancing to the music in the center of the group of sofas and tables that all the women are sitting around. Immediately, the women start digging into their purses to start pulling out dollar bills, twenties, or anything to tuck it into the waistband of my swim trunks.

I know my end target is Sloane. But, first, I give everyone else my attention. Sloane needs to see how the rest of her friends feel about me. She needs to see how desperate they are to just touch me, how they scream when I remove my shirt and reveal my rock-hard abs and strong chest. She needs to see what she would be missing if she said no instead of yes.

I strip down until I'm in nothing but my compression shorts that I wear under my swim trunks. All of the women's eyes in the room are filled with lust and desire. Including Paige, who has been coming and checking on everyone's drinks way more often than she should be. But she does nothing to stop me from stripping in a bar. I think because it has increased the number of drinks the rest of the women in the bar are ordering as they try to sneakily take a picture of me.

I have been ignoring Sloane the entire time I have been stripping. She thinks I'm doing this to hook up with a bridesmaid of my choosing. That, after this show, I will have my pick. She thinks she's safe. She is anything but safe.

"And, now, a special dance for the bride-to-be," I say.

Everyone hoots and hollers their agreement, and as I turn my attention to Sloane, it takes her a minute to realize that I'm talking about her. But, despite how she tries to hide it beneath a glare, I can see the lust and sin in her eyes. I can see the hint of temptation to do something that she knows she shouldn't do, that she would never forgive herself for. Still, it's there.

I grab Sloane's hand and drag her to the center of the circle. I have her take a seat on the edge of the low table in the center and then continue to dance around her and up against her. I give her an up close and personal view of my body, letting her get used to my body being close to her. When the music changes, I step it up a notch. I dance closer to her and eventually push her until she is lying on her back on the table.

I climb on top of the table and pretend to hump her without touching her, and when I hear the screams of the women around us, I know that I'm giving a good show.

I can see Sloane's anger growing right along with the lust. But I'm slightly disappointed in her. She's making this too easy for me. I want her to be in love with Wes. I want her to imagine herself with only him. When she falls in love with me and realizes that I can never love her in return, I want to know that it will ruin her. I want her to feel the kind of pain and devastation that she will never be able to return from. If I don't get that, then going after her now isn't going to be enough for me. Because I live for the devastation that I cause.

So, I up the ante when the music stops. I go in for a kiss because, if she isn't that in love with Wes anyway, she isn't going to be the woman I steal, and I might as well leave with a kiss.

But my lips barely brush hers before I feel the sting of a slap across my cheek, followed by a hard kick to the nuts. I roll off the table and crumple to the floor in unbearable pain as Sloane frowns over me along with all of her friends. Every one of their faces has turned from drunk happiness to anger. A few still have the lingering lust in their eyes, but most long pushed that thought out of their heads as soon as I went into the kiss.

"I'm marrying Wes. I love Wes. And any guy who thinks he can come in here and threaten my relationship with Wes deserves what's coming to him. Because Wes and I have been through too much to let some asshole like you who thinks he's God's gift to women to destroy that. It's not going to happen. And, if you do anything again, I'll make sure that your most prized possession is no longer attached to your body. Understand?"

I grin at Sloane. I can't help it. She loves him. It's music to my ears.

Sloane doesn't take my grin as a compliment though. She takes it as a grin from an arrogant asshole who is still going to try and get his way. And she's right.

Sloane grabs what is left of her whiskey and dumps it on my

head before I can react. I abruptly stand up and watch Sloane begin to walk out of the bar. But, before I can say anything else or run after her, another drink is thrown in my face. Followed by another and another until all of the women have thrown their drinks in my face. One woman kisses me on the lips before throwing her drink in my face and then slaps me after.

These women are crazy. But it's exactly what I want. Crazy, in-love women. I smile like a madman.

Luca walks over, laughing in my face.

"I thought you'd left," I say.

"I said I would leave after I watched you get thrown out. So, now, I can leave," he says.

"I didn't get thrown out."

He laughs again. "You're right. You just got a dozen drinks thrown in your face. That was much better than getting thrown out. I'm glad I stuck around to watch it happen. But what I don't understand is why you are grinning like an evil bastard. You do realize that you just got rejected by a dozen women, right?"

I nod. "I did." My grin curls up wider as I wipe my face off with my T-shirt, and then I put my swim trunks back on.

"Then, why are you still grinning? They won, and you lost. You look like a complete idiot."

"Because she loves him."

"Huh?"

"Sloane, the bride-to-be, loves her fiancé. That is going to make this so much sweeter when I finally steal her away."

Luca's smile drops.

I begin walking out of the bar, and Luca follows.

"I'm smiling because I think I just found my greatest challenge yet. Sloane."

FOUR

Asher

The sun begins to rise over the ocean as I sit in my hammock outside my shack on the beach. The bright yellow color that the sun brings is what I live for. Usually, before the sun starts to rise in the morning, I am already on the beach with my surfboard in hand. Early morning is the best time to catch some waves because very few people get up this early in the morning. The beach is empty as well as the ocean.

But today is the first time in years that I haven't woken before the sun with a surfboard in hand. The last time I remember missing a morning surf session was when I was sick with the flu. And, even then, I tried to get out of bed. I planned to go surfing that morning. My stomach just didn't agree with me, so I never left the bathroom that day.

I even go out surfing when the weather is less than perfect, which is rare for Hawaii, but still. I've surfed with the rain pouring down and lightning and thunder overhead.

Today though is the first day that I've chosen to do something else. I open my old laptop that I rarely, if ever, use and I type *Sloane* and *Hawaii* into the search bar. I don't have her last name, and I know it's a complete long shot, but maybe I'll get lucky. If not, I'm going to have to go back to the bar where I met her last night and convince Paige, the waitress, to tell me her last name.

It takes a minute for my Wi-Fi to connect and for the page to come up. But, finally, it does. I click on the first link and see Sloane's pretty, green eyes, luscious red lips, and shoulder-length blonde hair pop up on the screen.

I grin. This is too easy.

Her name is Sloane Hart. She runs a nonprofit called Kindness First with her grandmother. Actually, it's one of the biggest employers on the island and also has satellite locations around the world. I'm surprised I've never heard of her. But it's not like we run in the same circles. She's the complete opposite of me in fact.

I'm the devil. I destroy people's lives. She's an angel. She gives children food and a chance at life.

I pause for a second. I shouldn't do this. I shouldn't destroy a woman's life when she does so much good for the world.

What if, after I rip her heart out, she doesn't have the strength to continue her nonprofit work? What if she never leaves her house again? Becomes a hermit?

I would have not only destroyed her life, but also thousands of kids around the world. This is on a whole different level, even for me.

I stare back at the woman on the screen who looks so similar to so many local girls. In the picture, she is wearing a simple T-shirt with her company's logo and jeans. She's surrounded by kids that I'm sure she has been feeding. But, if you put her in a bikini, she would look just like every other girl on this island.

Except for one thing.

The twinkle in her eyes. It's different than anything I have ever seen before. It could just be this picture. The photographer could have just caught her eyes at just the right moment to catch the sunlight that caused her eyes to sparkle.

Or it could be her. I choose to believe it's Sloane causing the twinkle. The rest of her body language indicates as much.

And her smart mouth from last night tells me that she is used to being in control and is good at it. She's strong and kind. She'll survive. I might destroy her, but I have no doubt that she will keep the nonprofit going. And, if she doesn't, well, it's not my fault if thousands of children go hungry. I'm sure her job isn't that important anyway. Another organization would just take over caring for her kids.

I start reading article after article, trying to find out everything I can about Sloane Hart. She went to Harvard and majored in business. She graduated at the top of her class in fact. She grew up on the East Coast but would visit her grandmother here in Hawaii every summer. She moved here after graduation and has been working alongside her grandmother ever since. She met Wes at some point in college, but that is about all the articles say about Wes. He went to Harvard as well, so he can't be that stupid, but none of the articles talk about him running his own company or having any involvement in her company. They all just talk about their upcoming wedding. That's it.

I sigh when I finish reading the last article about Sloane that said much of the same as every other article about her. She's smart, loving, strong. The best person in the world to run a nonprofit organization. They all believe that, in the next five years, her nonprofit could become the largest in the world. She's that good at what she does. I've studied everything I can about her on paper, and I haven't found a weakness. Not a single one.

As far as I can tell, she doesn't have one. I grin, but this is exactly what I wanted. A challenge. And Sloane is not disappointing me there. This is exactly what I want.

I crack my neck from side to side as I begin to think of all my options to get into her life.

Apply for a job at her company? I shake my head. I don't have time for that, and as soon as she found out I was working for her, she would fire me.

Stalk her? Wouldn't work with Sloane. She'd call the police on me the second she spotted me.

Randomly run into her? She'd think I was stalking her.

My phone buzzes, interrupting my thoughts. I frown when I see the name on the screen. I answer though because I know, if I don't, she'll just keep calling me back.

"What?" I answer the phone.

"Well, hello to you, too. Why aren't you at the beach?" Shauna, my agent and basically my boss for all intents and purposes, asks.

I frown. "How do you know I'm not at the beach this morning? Are you spying on me? I'm allowed to take a break from surfing every once in a while."

She laughs. "I don't give a shit if you practice every day or not. All I care about is that you look good in your swim trunks and show up to the appearances and bookings we have given you. That's it."

"What are you talking about? I don't have an appearance or shoot today."

I can practically feel Shauna frowning on the other end of the line. That's how annoyed she is.

"I knew we shouldn't have hired a surfer. We pay you millions a year, and you can't even remember to show up when you're told. Even our basketball stars know how to show up even if they are still hungover from the night before. But, no, we decided to go with a surfer. Surfers are cool, are in right now. A surfer will help our brand. Right now, all I think is, we are paying you too goddamn much to not show up when you're told."

"Shauna, I'm sorry you're having a shitty day or PMSing or whatever is going on with you. But I was never told about an appearance for today." I check my calendar and email quickly to make sure, but there is nothing there.

I grin because I'm right, and Shauna is wrong.

"Shit, you're right. Why the fuck do you have to be right?"

"Because I'm the devil."

She sighs. "That, you are. Regardless of whose fault it is, I need you on the beach in ten minutes, or the cushiony paycheck we pay you every month will go away."

I laugh. "No, it won't. This is your fault. You screwed up, not me. And, if you think I care about the money, you are wrong."

"Goddamn it, Asher! Just get your ass down to the beach now. It's not like you have anything better to do. You surf; that's it. That's your entire life. So, just do it."

"And what will you do for me?"

"I won't kill you. Now, go! You need this job anyway. Even though you still win plenty of events, you are getting less sponsorships because of your reputation with women, which we need to discuss later. You aren't a great image for many people's brands. So, just be happy that you are getting any work."

I frown and then hear her mumble something about surfers and how she'll never work with a surfer again before she realizes she never ended the call. When I hear the beeping sound, indicating that she did hang up, I get up out of my hammock and return my laptop to my shack. The laptop was secondhand and cost less than a hundred dollars, so it's not like anyone is going to come in and steal it.

Shauna forgets that I don't care about money, or maybe she just doesn't remember. As long as I can buy beer and food, I'm good. I could easily make money by flipping burgers for a few hours each day and still have plenty of time to spend most of my day surfing.

I change into swim trunks and then climb into my truck that already has my surfboard in the back.

I begin driving toward the best surfing spot on the island. Shauna never said where I was supposed to go or what the appearance was. But I know where she is talking about. And, no matter what the appearance is, I'll need to be in swim trunks, or they will tell me what they want me to wear.

And maybe a distraction away from Sloane for a couple of hours isn't such a bad idea. It will help me to get my thoughts in order so that I can form a plan of attack for later.

I pull up to the spot on the beach ten minutes later. And I jump out of my truck and find Shauna looking as sassy as ever in her heels and dress. She starts walking toward me, and I laugh as her heels sink in the sand.

"Are you ever going to learn to dress appropriately for the beach?" I ask her as I cock my head to one side.

She frowns. "I don't have time for your crap today, Asher."

"Honestly, I think you are the only person in the world who hates the beach. Most people would love to have your job and be able to hang out in Hawaii all day."

She rolls her eyes. "Today, you are giving surf lessons."

I frown. "Surf lessons? Really? That's the big money-making opportunity that I was going to cost us if I didn't show up today?"

Shauna motions to the camera crew behind her. "We are filming it for a couple of ads, and the guys are paying big bucks to have you teach them."

I groan. "You couldn't have at least found a group of women who needed surf lessons?"

"That's not what we are going for. We want you to show that surfing can make any guy look cool."

"You know women with boobs sell a lot better."

She laughs. "It sells better to *guys*. But we aren't trying to sell to guys. We are trying to sell to *women*. And what better way to sell to women than with a bunch of hot guys who are single?"

"Don't you think we will come across as gay?"

She shrugs. "Maybe, but women also like knowing they can turn a hot gay guy straight. Or at least fantasize about it. It doesn't matter. Just be hot and teach these guys how to surf. They agreed to let us film them, and they all happen to be hot as well, so lucky us."

I frown. "I should have stayed home."

"Then, you wouldn't have gotten paid. Now, go teach those guys how to surf."

She swats my ass as I walk by.

"I don't care about the money, and I'm pretty sure that was sexual harassment!" I yell back as I jog toward the group of guys awkwardly holding surfboards at the edge of the water.

"Then, sue me!" she shouts back.

I smile.

I turn my attention to the idiots standing on the beach. "I'm Asher. I guess I'll be teaching you how to surf today."

A blonde guy with a short haircut and, I hate to say, a fit body sticks out his hand. "I'm Wes."

My lips curl up just a little at the mention of his name. "Nice to meet you, Wes."

"And these are my cousins and groomsmen, Elijah and Cody."

I shake each of their hands.

"I'm his best man," Elijah says.

"Don't let him fool you. I'm his best man," Cody says.

Wes rolls his eyes. "The best man spot is still up for grabs."

"And the spot of the bride?" I ask.

"That's taken by Sloane Hart. You might have heard of her.

She runs Kindness First, a nonprofit whose headquarters are located here on the island."

I shake my head. "Never heard of her. But you sound like a lucky man."

"I am," Wes says, smiling like an idiot.

That's when I realize what Sloane's weakness is. Wes. Wes is her weakness. It's clear he doesn't have a lot of guy friends if he brought only his cousins, and he doesn't clearly have a best man. That means, there is a spot open for me. I can become his friend. His best man even. That will ensure I get to spend plenty of time with Sloane. And Sloane won't be able to turn me away because I'll be Wes's best friend. That's my way in. Through Wes.

"So, have any of you surfed before?"

All three shake their heads.

I put on a fake smile. "Well, let's see what you've got."

"You aren't going to teach us how to stand on the board on the ground first?" Elijah asks.

I raise an eyebrow. "Do you really want to spend all day jumping up on a surfboard on the sand, or do you want to learn how to surf?"

"Well...I-I..." Elijah stutters.

I roll my eyes. "If you were looking for a babysitter to teach you, then you came to the wrong place. I believe in learning from doing, not pretending. I'm the best surfer in the world, currently ranked number one. If you want to learn from the best, then you don't get to question my methods. If you aren't willing to take my terms, then stop wasting my time."

Wes smiles. "Teach us your ways, oh great one."

I nod. "Good. I'll get my board and meet you out there. Lie on your board and swim as far out into the ocean as you can."

"Shouldn't we wait for you?" Cody asks.

"Don't worry; I'll catch up."

I jog back to my truck to grab my board, happy that this has taken such a good turn. The only thing better would have been if Sloane herself were asking for lessons, but something tells me that, even if Sloane didn't know how to surf, she wouldn't be the type to ask for lessons. She would be the type to learn how to surf and be great at it the first time out. She wouldn't need an instructor.

I grab my board and then begin jogging back to the beach. I see the cameraman aiming his camera at me as I jog. I can't imagine how they are going to turn this into a commercial, but if I can buddy up to Wes while getting paid to do it, then I'm not going to complain.

As I jog back down the beach with my board in hand, I glance out at them floundering in the ocean, seemingly barely moving at all, as wave after wave crashes down on them. I wouldn't have brought first-time surfers to this beach, but I know why my sponsors chose this spot. It has the best waves and lighting. They'll just be lucky to get a shot of any of them up on a surfboard. Although maybe they just want an ad of a bunch of hot guys hanging out and looking stupid while I surf.

Wes is the only one who is making any progress at all, though he isn't that far ahead of the rest of them.

I run into the water with my surfboard and then dive under the first wave. I swim hard, kicking my feet to propel me forward, and then finally come up for air several feet in front of Wes.

"Dive under the next wave!" I shout to Wes.

I sit on top of the waves for the next one so that I can see how he does. He tries but ends up coming up, quickly coughing up the salty water.

I chuckle. "Try again. Blow out through your nose this time as you dive, so you don't get a nose full of water."

Wes tries again, and this time, he makes it to me before he comes back up.

"Not bad," I say as he breathes heavily next to me.

"Yeah, I'm awesome. I can dive underwater and hold my breath for five seconds. I was born to surf," Wes says sarcastically.

I laugh. "Well, you are doing better than Tweedle Dee and Tweedle Dum back there."

Wes laughs as we both stare back at his cousins, who have barely moved from the edge of the beach.

"I guess we should wait for them," I say.

"Nah, I need a break from them."

I nod. "All right, so one more dive, and you should be in position. This time, dive down and kick hard until you can't hold your breath anymore. That should get you on the other side of the swell. Then, we'll have you up and surfing."

He laughs.

"And dive," I say.

We both dive down into the water. When I come up for air, I see that Wes has, too, but he's going to have to take one or two more dives down to get to where I am. I wait patiently as he does. When he finally reaches me, he is breathing heavily. He's in decent shape, but the ocean definitely takes a different toll on the body if you aren't used to it.

"So, why do you want to learn how to surf anyway?" I ask.

"My fiancée. She's spent many summers here, and if we are going to live here full-time after we get married, I figured I'd better learn how to surf. I know she loves it even if she rarely makes time to surf anymore. I want to be able to do something with her that she enjoys and not look like a total imbecile."

I nod. "I think you are going to need more than one lesson today to accomplish that."

"Yeah, well, I was told you'd only do the one."

"I think I could fit you into my schedule for the next couple of weeks."

"That would be great."

I look back to the camera crew, who is growing impatient. "I need to get up on the board to ensure I get paid. After I go, give it your best shot. You're going to fall if you even get up, but I think that is what they are wanting."

Wes nods. "Yeah, I figured."

"But don't worry; I'll have you surfing. Just give me a week or two."

I see the next wave coming. It's not perfect, but then nothing ever is. I wink at Wes, and I take off with the wave.

I don't have to think as I surf; I just do. I've done this so many times before, and this wave is nothing compared to the larger waves that I often surf. Still, I respect the wave, the ocean. I know that, every time I come out here, I'm putting my life at risk. That this could all be over if I'm not careful. So, I try to keep my thoughts on what I'm doing and not on Sloane. Not on the plan that has practically fallen into my lap.

I reach the shore and jump off the board before I remember that I'm being filmed. I make sure to smile as I kick the board up with my foot and then carry it all the way up the beach. I turn my attention back to Wes, who is sitting on his board, looking completely clueless and completely terrified.

I watch the next wave come, but it is going to be much too strong for him. "Hold off till the next one!" I shout.

He nods and tries to maintain his position as the next wave comes. It really doesn't matter which wave he tries. I doubt he even manages to stand on the board his first time out.

I watch as another wave begins. "This one, Wes! Start paddling and then try to stand!" I shout.

Wes begins paddling and then starts trying to climb up onto the board. His timing is off, but somehow, he muscles his way up until he is somewhat upright. Then, he immediately falls over as a wave crashes down on him.

He comes up for air a couple of seconds later, looking a bit dazed but otherwise fine. He slowly makes his way back to the beach and then falls to the ground.

"I don't know how you are able to make that look so easy. I don't think I'll ever be able to stand up on the board," Wes says, panting hard.

"Well, you won't ever be able to do what I just did unless you plan on devoting your next twenty years to surfing. But I can at least get you upright your next time out."

I extend my hand to him, and he takes it and stands up.

"Same place tomorrow?" Wes asks.

I glance over at the police cruiser that is creeping by far too slowly, staring at us.

I laugh. "No. We are going to try a much tamer beach next time."

It's taken me three weeks to get Wes to stand on a board and do anything that resembles surfing. It has been much longer of an investment than I initially planned. I thought one week, maybe two, and then I'd not only have him surfing, but he would also have made me his best man. Apparently, I'm better at making friends with women than with men.

"I told you I would have you surfing," I say to Wes as he trudges up to his car.

"Woohoo! That was awesome! I can't wait to show Sloane on our honeymoon."

I place my surfboard into the back of my truck. "Where are you going on your honeymoon?"

"Australia and then New Zealand. Sloane has always wanted to go. She's the adventurous type. She wants to surf, scuba dive the Great Barrier Reef, hike in the forests. I, on the other hand, just want to avoid being eaten by anything and kick back and enjoy the food. She'll be impressed though that I took surfing lessons and can sort of surf now."

I smile every time Wes talks about Sloane. I can't help it. I've learned a lot about her from my time with him. And everything that I have learned makes me want to claim her more. Makes me want her more. And this new fact is not any different.

"I think, with a little more practice, you are definitely going to impress her."

Wes opens the door to his car. "Hey, you want to come out with us tonight?"

I raise an eyebrow. "I don't want to be a third wheel."

Wes laughs. "I didn't mean, me and Sloane. I meant, me and the guys. They are kind of throwing me an informal bachelor party tonight. You should come."

"I don't want to intrude."

"Oh, come on. Don't leave me alone with my cousins. They are the absolute worst. I need at least one normal guy who is on my side tonight."

"All right, fine. I'll come hit the bars with you tonight. But you owe me for putting up with your cousins."

"First round is on me."

I nod. "Done."

I get to the saddest-looking bar on the island, where Wes texted me to meet them. I frown as I stand outside the building that looks like it could collapse at any minute. I'm not one to judge a book by its cover. After all, I'm nothing like what I appear on the outside. But this is absolutely ridiculous. If they weren't going to pick a strip club, they could have at least picked a clean bar that had average-looking waitresses who were scantily clad.

I shake my head. If I convince them to go to any other bar tonight, I'll be considered a savior after Wes tries one drink in this place. Tonight, I need him to start thinking of me as one of his best friends. I need to start finding a way to connect with Sloane. I need to start sneaking into her life. And, if Wes isn't that way, then I will need to find another.

I walk into the bar, still dressed in swim trunks, a T-shirt, and sandals. I don't have to look long to find them. The three of them are sitting at the edge of the bar, all looking sad. They are the only ones in here besides an older gentleman who is behind the bar, fixing them drinks.

"Cheer up, guys. The party is here," I say, heading over to them.

Wes smiles when he sees me, but Elijah and Cody both give me a glare that is a mix between anger and annoyance.

I don't bother to pull up a chair because we definitely aren't staying here.

"Close out your tabs, boys, and let me show you how a local parties in Hawaii."

Wes immediately jumps up, but Cody and Elijah both continue to frown.

"We are in charge of the bachelor party, not you. We will decide when and if we want to go elsewhere," Cody says.

I raise an eyebrow. "Well, you've chosen one of the worst dumps on the island. But, if you want to stay, be my guest. Or we could go to a bar that actually has decent drinks and chicks, most scantily clad and likely ready for a good time."

"Aw, come on, guys. It's my night. I appreciate you guys trying your best, but Asher knows the island better than any of us. Let's give him a try."

"Fine," Cody says.

I pull out my wallet and throw some cash down so that they might like me a little better. Although I think it does the opposite of helping. I don't really care if they like me though. I just need to convince Wes, which is easy since he's comparing me to them.

I throw my arm over Wes's shoulder. "Come on, let's go get you drunk and see some naked chicks."

Three hours later, and I have succeeded in getting everyone drunk, and we have had a string of naked women coming all night. I might have succeeded in my mission.

Cody is passed out at the bar, clueless to the fact that he is lying in spilled beer. Elijah has spent the last half hour in the restroom, most likely vomiting. And Wes is a stumbling mess, no longer speaking in coherent sentences.

I sigh. Why the hell I thought I wanted to spend an evening with just the guys is beyond me. I don't even like spending time with Luca, and he's about the only person on earth who can stand me.

Unfortunately, there aren't many cab options on the island this late in the evening, so it is up to me to either get them home or leave them here. I should leave their asses here. They are all grown men who can take care of themselves. But I keep picturing Sloane.

I smile, thinking of her. There is one benefit to everyone being drunk out of their minds.

"Come on, Wes. It's time to let your best man take you home," I say, putting his arm around my shoulders and helping him to stand up.

Wes smiles as I guide him outside to my truck. I knew well enough not to get drunk tonight.

I throw Wes in the truck before I decide I'd better go get Elijah and Cody.

"Don't tell Elijah and Cody that you're my best man. They'll be mad," Wes says, slurring every other word out of his mouth.

"Don't worry. It will be our secret," I say before slamming the door shut.

Finally, I think as I go back to get the other two drunk assholes.

I can't put up with these guys any longer without at least getting a glimpse of Sloane.

Phase one is complete. Now, it's on to the more fun phase. Enticing Sloane.

SIX

Asher

It feels strange to wake up and not be teaching Wes for once. But it's also incredibly fucking nice. I jump out of bed and glance out my window. The sun is just starting to rise over the ocean, and it looks like it is going to be the best goddamn day.

Wes already gave me a schedule of events I need to be at as his best man over the next month. I don't have any events that I need to be at for my sponsors.

Today, I'm a free man. I can just surf.

I slip into my swim trunks and don't bother to throw on a shirt. Then, I run out the door and get in my truck to head to my favorite spot on the beach.

When I get there, I jump out of the truck and grab my surfboard before running toward the ocean.

"Hey, man!"

I freeze and do my best not to groan.

I turn and face Wes. "Hey, what are you doing here? I thought we were done with lessons."

"We are. Just wanted to show my fiancée what I'd learned."

I see it in her eyes the second she spots me. Immediate

recognition, regret, and anger. She recovers quickly and tucks a loose strand of her blonde hair behind her ear as Wes turns to grab her hand.

"This is my fiancée, Sloane Hart. Sloane, this is Asher Calder," Wes says.

Sloane holds out her hand to me, and I shake it with a mischievous grin on my face—or at least, that's how I imagine she views my grin.

Sloane smiles politely and shakes my hand. "I've tried teaching Wes how to surf many times, so I'm still not convinced that he has learned how to actually surf, even by someone as experienced with surfing as you are," she says as she retracts her hand.

Wes laughs.

I cock my head to one side as I study Sloane. She looked up who I was, or she'd already known who I was. That has me even more intrigued with her.

"Are you underestimating my surfing skills?" I instinctively move toward her, unable to resist closing the distance between us.

Sloane holds tight to Wes, like he is going to be able to stop me.

"No, just your teaching skills and Wes's lack of coordination."

Wes and Sloane laugh together, like most couples do. Like they share a secret no one else knows. Seeing them happy together just makes me want to rip them apart even more.

"Well, Wes, you'd better go out there and prove her wrong for both of our sakes. I wouldn't want her to find either of us lacking."

Sloane frowns every time I speak, but the second Wes looks at her, a fake smile appears on her lips. It's entertaining really, watching her.

Wes kisses her on the lips, and I study them both. When Wes kisses, he closes his eyes and lets her into his soul. When Sloane kisses, it's clear that she isn't fully in the moment. Her eyes don't close all the way, and her lips don't part all the way to let him in or so that he can fully claim her mouth with his.

Sloane gently pushes Wes away. She tries to hide it. She tries to make it seem like she wants nothing more than to be kissed by Wes all day. It's clear that me being here makes her uncomfortable.

Wes smiles at Sloane, so oblivious and in love that he can't even tell that she had issues with his kiss. He grabs his surfboard and then begins walking toward the water.

He pauses just before going in. "You coming, Asher?"

"Nope, this is all you."

Wes runs into the water with his surfboard in hand and begins paddling out.

Sloane folds her arms across her chest and watches Wes with laser focus. So much focus that I am able to move until I'm standing right next to her.

"He's good, isn't he?" I say into her ear.

She jumps.

I lean back, away from her ear, as she turns to me.

"What are you doing? Why did you give Wes surf lessons?"

"Are you accusing me of setting this all up so that I could see you again?"

"Yes, that is exactly what I'm accusing you of."

I fold my arms across my chest and watch her eyes linger on my abs for a second before looking me in the eye again.

I laugh. "As luck would have it, fate stepped in. My sponsors arranged the lessons, not me. It would seem the world thinks we should be together."

"You're an asshole, a douche bag, a bastard, a—"

I laugh. "Is that the best you've got?"

She narrows her eyes. "I'm engaged! What kind of man thinks I'd be willing to have a one-night stand with him, a complete stranger, on a normal night, much less when I'm about to be married? There isn't a name so bad to describe what you are."

I shrug. "At least none that you can call me from your pretty, little mouth."

She glares at me, and I know she means it as a warning that I have no doubt she would follow through on if I tried anything, but all I can think is that I want to see that same passion in her eyes when I kiss her. I want to see how angry she would be if I kissed her right now. I want to feel that anger with just the tiniest hint of desire. Because I know that, once she got a taste of me, no matter how much she loved Wes, she would keep coming back for more.

"You'd better turn your attention to your fiancé. You wouldn't want him to see that you couldn't take your eyes off me when you were supposed to be watching him."

Sloane huffs but doesn't say another word as she turns her attention to Wes, who is now sitting on his surfboard, waiting for a wave. I, however, don't take my eyes off of her. And, even though she tries her best to fix her gaze on Wes, she still looks at me out of the corner of her eye.

"Oh my God...he's..." Sloane says.

I reluctantly tear my eyes from Sloane to look out at Wes. He's now standing on a surfboard. He's a little shaky but standing fairly well as he glides down toward us.

"How did you do it?" Sloane looks at me with wide eyes.

"I'm a good teacher, and your fiancé isn't that bad of a learner."

Sloane turns back to Wes, who is still up on the surfboard. "He's a terrible learner. He has no coordination and no athletic ability really. He occasionally runs and lifts weights, but beyond that, nothing. I've been trying to get him up on a surfboard for years. How did you do it?"

"Like I told you, I'm a pro. I'm very good at what I do. I never lose. I always get what I want. If I want to get someone up on a surfboard, I will. And, if I want to get you in my bed, I will."

"I'm thankful to you for helping Wes, but I'm very happy that I will be the first time you lose. You will never find me in your bed. In fact, you will never see either of us again. It's clear that Wes doesn't need your services any longer, and we still haven't decided where we will be making our permanent home after we are married, but I can assure you, it won't be anywhere near you."

I lean in close to her ear and smell the flowery perfume she is wearing. "Actually, you'll be seeing a lot of me."

Wes falls off the board, and Sloane's mouth falls open as she watches him hit the rough water.

"What do you mean?"

"Just that, since I'm Wes's best man, I expect that you will be seeing a lot of me. So, make sure you are strong enough to resist my charm if you are going to make promises about being the first time I lose."

Wes runs toward us, carrying his surfboard. "What do you think?" he asks.

"You were incredible. I can't believe you were able to do that," Sloane answers. She kisses him on the lips, but it's a chaste kiss.

"I'm ready to go again. Want to join me?" Wes asks Sloane.

Sloane looks over at me and then back to Wes. "No, I'm not feeling the best. I'd rather just sit here and watch you."

That's when I notice the strings of Sloane's bikini sticking out from the neck of her T-shirt. I'd love to see her in nothing but a bikini.

"You going to join me and make me look like a fool?" Wes asks.

I laugh. "Well, I did come here to train, but you don't need me to make you look like a fool. You already do that by yourself."

Wes laughs and starts heading back out into the water. I turn back to my truck and grab my own surfboard.

I walk slowly past Sloane, knowing full well that the only reason she didn't take Wes up on his offer to go out surfing with him is because she wanted to stay back and have it out with me. I raise an eyebrow as I walk, daring her to talk to me.

"You can't be Wes's best man," she hisses.

"And why not?"

"Because you are a horrible person who is just doing this to try and sleep with me."

I grin. "That's exactly why I'm doing this. But it's also exactly why you can't do a damn thing about it. You love Wes, and Wes chose me as his best man. And, if you really think you can resist me, there is no harm in giving Wes what he wants."

Her mouth drops open, but no words come out. I take off toward the ocean, knowing that her eyes are on me. She can't help but watch. And, when she sees how awesome I am at surfing, how I glide over the water like it's in my control, she will want me to control her in the same way.

SEVEN

Asher

I step foot inside the building that Wes texted me in order to get fitted for my tux or whatever he, his cousins, and I are wearing at the wedding. It's a small building jam-packed with tuxes and men's formal attire.

I spot Wes in the back, standing alone, talking to one of the salespeople.

I grin. "Thank God it's just us. I wasn't sure if I could deal with your cousins today," I say, bumping fists with Wes.

"If you want to avoid them, then you'd better try on your tux quickly. They'll be here any minute."

I frown. "Let's get this started then."

"This is my best man, Asher," Wes says to the salesperson.

"I'm Luther. I just need to take a few measurements, and I'll have you try on a couple of jackets and pants. Then, I'll get you out of here," Luther says.

"Excellent," I say.

Luther begins measuring every inch of me. Well, every inch, except for the one part of my body where size really matters—at least, I think so. When he's done, he thinks for a moment and then grabs a couple of jackets and pants.

He carries them into a dressing room. "Try them on. I might have to make some adjustments with the jacket. You will have to go up a size or two to fit your biceps, but then we will need to take it in at the waist to fit everywhere else."

I head into the dressing room and begin trying on the first pair of pants. It feels strange to wear anything this formal. I haven't worn anything this formal since—

I stop thinking. I will not let my mind go there. Not today.

I try the jacket on over my T-shirt. It's a bit snug, so I try the larger size and then step out of the dressing room.

"Just as I suspected. To fit you in the arms and chest, you need the bigger jacket, but we are going to have to take it in to make it fit your waist."

Luther starts messing with the jacket, trying to ensure it will fit, while I stand there, sweating in the thick material.

"Did you say where you are getting married, Wes?" I ask.

"The beach," he answers.

It's like I suspected.

"Are you sure you are going to want to wear tuxes on the beach in summertime in Hawaii? You do know it gets hot here, right?"

Wes frowns. "I didn't really think about it, but now that you mention it—"

"I already told you that the tuxes were stupid. You should just wear khakis and a dress shirt," Sloane says, seemingly appearing from nowhere.

I smile when I see her. I didn't realize that she would be here, but it makes my day so much better.

"Khakis and a dress shirt, I could get behind as well," I say.

I wink at Sloane. She just rolls her eyes and focuses her attention on Wes.

"I need to think about it. I'm not sure khakis are formal enough."

Sloane throws her hands up in defeat. "You don't have time to decide. You have to decide today."

"Then, tuxes. This is going to be in every newspaper in the country. It will be going in countless magazines. I want to look like I'm getting married, not like I'm a bum hanging out at the beach one day."

"We are going to be sweating like pigs in these, man. Just think about that," I say.

"I don't care. It's just for a couple of hours. It won't be that bad," Wes says.

"Don't say I didn't tell you so," Sloane says.

"What do you think of the fit, Ms. Hart?" Luther asks.

Sloane walks over to me and pretends to care about how my jacket and pants are fitting. "Seems to fit fine, but I'm guessing he'll want it a bit looser with all the sweating he will be doing."

I laugh.

Wes frowns.

"Oh, come on. I'm only kidding," Sloane says.

Wes takes Sloane in his arms. "I just want everything to be perfect for you, baby. I don't care about a little sweat."

I can't help but laugh to myself when Wes calls Sloane baby. She seems like anything but a baby to me.

Wes's phone rings, and he steps away to answer it.

"We need to talk," Sloane says, hissing through her teeth in a similar way that she did two days ago when she spoke to me on the beach.

"Then, talk," I say, adjusting the jacket, and looking at myself in the mirror. I look strange in a tux and not just because I'm wearing a T-shirt under the jacket, but also because it is the complete opposite of who I am. I hate fancy things.

I see Sloane staring at me in the mirror, and then her eyes

dart to Luther and back to me. I smile. She wants to talk to me alone.

"I don't have lunch plans. Would you and Wes like to join me for lunch?" I ask.

Wes walks back over. "What is this about lunch?"

"I thought we should all go have lunch together, so I can get to know your fiancée a little better."

"I wish I could join you, but that was Elijah. His car broke down. He needs me to pick him and Cody up and bring them to the tux fitting. But you two should go. It would make things easier if you two got along," Wes says.

"I'll just get changed, and then we can go. I'll let you pick the place," I say before heading into the dressing room to change.

I put my swim trunks, T-shirt, and sandals back on while I listen to Wes and Sloane whisper to each other. I can't make out what they are saying, but it doesn't sound like happy whispering.

When I open the curtain separating me from them, they stop and both put fake smiles on their faces.

"Ready to go?" I ask Sloane.

She nods.

I sit down at the booth across from Sloane in the swanky restaurant she chose to have lunch at. I don't have to open the menu to know that the prices are outrageous. Most places on the island are expensive. This is just over the top.

I'm not opposed to having a good meal or even going to a swanky place on occasion but not for lunch, especially when I doubt we are even going to be able to make it through this meal.

Sloane is wearing a pale yellow dress and heels today. She looks hot as hell, and it makes me want to take her into the restroom and rip the dress off of her. I won't. That's not my game. But I can still imagine it.

"What are you grinning about?" she asks.

"You don't want to know."

"I do. Otherwise, I wouldn't have asked."

"You, naked."

She rolls her eyes. "You really are a one-track-mind kind of man, aren't you?"

I shrug. "So, what did you want to say?"

"I want you to leave me alone."

I smile and lean back in the booth, extending my arm on the back of the cushion. A nicely dressed woman at the table over gives me a disgusted stare.

"Now, who has a one-track mind?"

"Can I get you anything to drink?"

"White wine," Sloane says, clearly needing a drink to get through this meal.

"Water," I say.

"That's all you want? I'm buying," she says.

I laugh. "You think I can't afford to buy myself a drink? Really?" I shake my head. If I hadn't already decided to go after her, this would have been a major turn-off—her thinking she was better than me because she dressed better. "I'll have water," I say again to the waiter. "I have a training session after I leave here."

Sloane doesn't blush in embarrassment, like I expected. She just sits there, unfazed by me calling her out. She just went up a few notches in my opinion.

"Are you ready to order lunch?" the waiter asks.

I raise my eyebrows at Sloane. "Do you think you can make it through a whole meal with me?"

"I'll have the grilled chicken salad," she says.

Of course she orders a salad, like any other thin girl on the planet would when eating with a man she secretly wanted to bang. If she truly wasn't interested in me, she would have ordered the burger or pizza or anything that had carbs.

"Pepperoni pizza," I say.

The waiter leaves, and then it's just Sloane and me.

Another woman passing by the table stares at me, and at first, she seems disgusted that they would let someone wearing swim trunks into the restaurant. But then, when she looks up further and sees my body and my crooked grin that I know turns her on, she doesn't seem to mind so much.

"Do you always wear swim trunks everywhere you go?"

"Yes. Why wouldn't I? I live in Hawaii, and I'm a surfer."

Her eyes study me, and I know she's wishing that I wasn't wearing anything either. That she would love to see what was beneath the swim trunks.

"You can't be in the wedding. You can't be Wes's best man."

"Sure I can. I have the date cleared and everything. I don't have any competitions or any events I have to attend for my sponsors, and I don't have any women to pick up that day. So, I will definitely be making your wedding."

The waiter brings our drinks. I expect Sloane to slug down her wine, needing liquid courage or strength to deal with me. She doesn't. She sips it coolly, like she deals with propositions from men every day and she just has to come to the right terms to get me to say I'm not coming to her wedding. If that's the way she wants to play, then fine, I'll play along.

"What do you want? Really? You can't think that I'm going to sleep with you. It's just a fun game for you to try. You could probably have dozens of women in the amount of time it would take you to chase me. Is that what you like? The chase. Chasing women you can't have? Is that what turns you on?"

I cock my head to the side. "Something like that."

"What do I need to do to get you to go away? How much money?"

I laugh. "I don't want money. I have too much as it is."

"Then, what do you want?"

"Go out with me."

"What?" she asks, her eyes growing wide.

"Go. Out. On. A. Date. With. Me."

She slowly shakes her head. "I'm married, remember?"

I cock my head and smile. "I thought you were just engaged. Did you two secretly get married, or do you already feel like an old married couple?"

She frowns. "You know what I meant. I'm about to be married. Almost-married women don't go out on dates."

"But you aren't most married women. One date, and I'll leave you alone. One date, and if after the date you still want me to leave, I will. I'll tell Wes that I can't be in the wedding. Something came up, like a surf competition or event that I couldn't get out of. Just one date."

"No."

"Think about it before you say no."

"No."

I laugh. "If you don't go out with me, I'm going to drive you crazy. I'll be at every wedding event that you have. The rehearsal, the wedding, the reception. I'll be there, haunting you. And don't think you'll get rid of me after the wedding. I'll still be there. I'm Wes's best friend after all. I'll be at every family event. I'll start a double-date night with you and Wes. I'll be there every week. I'll be there after the birth of your first child and every birthday afterward. I'll hit on you every time."

"No." She narrows her eyes in defiance this time before taking a sip of her wine, like she thinks she is going to be the one to win this.

She won't. She forgets, I never lose. Ever.

"You'll always wonder if you don't go on a date with me. I'll haunt your dreams. You'll always wonder, *What if?* What if you were wrong about Wes and I was the guy for you?"

"No."

"If you go out with me, you can confirm to yourself that I'm the asshole you think I am. You'll never have to wonder."

"I don't wonder."

"Yes, you do. If you didn't have the tiniest hint of wonder about me, you wouldn't even be bothering with me. You wouldn't be here."

"No."

"My body will haunt you. You'll always wonder about my body, my abs, and other things," I say winking.

"No. Wes has great abs," she says. But there is a hint of seduction in her voice. A hint that she knows what I'm saying is true. That she wants me.

"Not like mine. He's nothing like me."

"No, because you are the devil."

I nod. "True. But, if you truly loved Wes, you'd have nothing to lose by going out with me. In fact, you would be saving Wes from a monster like me."

Sloane takes another sip of wine and clears her throat. "Okay."

I smile smugly. "That didn't sound like a yes to me. Will you go out on a date with me?"

"Let's get one thing straight. I'm going out with you to get rid of you. And the second the date is over and I tell you I'm done is the second you leave my life forever. Got it? I don't play games."

"So, is that a yes?"

She crosses her arms.

"I need to hear you say it, or the deal is void. I need to hear you say that you will go out on a date with me. A real date."

She rolls her arms. "Yes, I will go out on a date with you."

I grin. "Good."

The waiter brings us our lunch, which is good because I am starving and really do need to go to training after we get finished here. I dig into the pizza that is in front of me, eating quickly. After my second slice, I look up and see Sloane staring at me.

"What?"

"You're a pig."

I shrug. "I'm hungry. I assume you are planning on leaving now that you got what you wanted, and I have places to be. So, what if I eat a little fast? We aren't on a date right now, so what does it matter?"

She rolls her eyes for the millionth time it seems since we sat down at this table.

"You should eat, too. You'll need your strength for our date this weekend."

She huffs. "I'll have days to gather my strength to deal with you on our date."

"You should eat anyway."

She starts eating her salad while I finish off my pizza. And then I chuckle to myself.

"Now what?"

I shake my head. "I just can't believe you said yes."

EIGHT

Asher

I enter the lobby of the fancy condo building that Sloane lives in. I stare up at the large ceiling that goes up in the center to what must be the top floor with all the other entrances to the rooms surrounding the center. The whole building seems extravagant. Everything is wrapped in gold or silver. Flowers decorate the main floor lobby, but there isn't a dead flower in sight, making it clear that the flowers are pruned and replaced on a regular basis. There is a lot of wealth in this place.

Too much wealth if you ask me.

I walk to the elevator and am stopped by a nicely dressed man in a suit.

"Who are you here to see, sir?" the man asks politely, blocking me from entering the elevator without telling him first.

I look down at my khaki shorts and button-down shirt that is open at the collar. I thought I would dress up a bit for our date tonight, but looking at myself now and where I am, I should have dressed up more because Sloane is a princess who no doubt lives on the top floor of her castle. Despite working for a nonprofit she inherited, she makes plenty of money and expects to live with the finer things in life.

"I'm here to see Sloane Hart," I answer.

"And your name is?"

"Asher Calder."

I expect him to request to see my ID before he will let me up. But, to my surprise, he pushes the button for the elevator, and he steps aside to let me in as the doors open. He steps inside and presses the button for floor number ten.

"Ms. Hart's place is the first door on your left when you exit the elevator. Have a good day, Mr. Calder," he says before leaving the elevator.

I run my hand through my hair as the elevator makes its way up. I can't believe people live like this. I know he is here mostly for security purposes, but it still seems ridiculous that she lives in a place where somebody stands at the elevator and pushes a button for her whenever she wants to go up. As if she is incapable of pressing a button. It's a good thing I don't want her forever because we don't belong together. She wants a fancy life, full of finer things, while I want to live with as few things as possible.

I shake my head at the thought of ever imagining myself with anyone for more than a couple of months. That's not my style. I don't do the boyfriend or girlfriend thing, and I don't imagine ever getting married.

The doors open, and I step off and knock on her door. I wait longer than I expected. She doesn't answer right away even though, if anything, I'm a few minutes late. I pull out my phone, ready to text her with the number that Wes gave me, to see if she is still coming or if she changed her mind, when she opens the door.

She's wearing a beautiful pale blue sundress that, to my surprise, has more cleavage than I would have thought she would wear for a date that isn't really a date. Her blonde hair is curled, but it's her eyes that have my complete attention.

It's clear that she has been crying. Despite trying to dry her eyes, her eyeliner and mascara are smudged, and her eyes are still a bit swollen and red.

"So, where are we going?" Sloane asks, plastering a fake smile on her face.

I frown. "What's wrong?"

Her smile falters. "Oh, nothing. Just allergies."

"Don't lie to me."

"You're one to talk. You lie all the time."

"No, I don't. I have made my intentions very clear to you. I want you. In my bed. As soon as possible. Now, what is wrong?"

"My grandmother died."

I feel her pain immediately. It's clear that she was close to her grandmother.

"I'm so sorry."

I see the tears forming in her eyes again, but she holds them back, not letting me fully see her pain.

"You should be with Wes tonight. We can reschedule, or I can..." I can't quite convince myself to say that I'd leave her alone. Because I can't promise it. I want this too much. I want to steal her heart and know it's mine and not his. I want to be the cause of her pain. But I'm not devil enough to do it when her grandmother just died.

"Wes is gone," she says.

"Gone?"

"He's in LA on business."

"Does he know?"

"Yes," she whispers.

"Are you going to be able to forgive him for not being here?"

"I have to."

"No, you don't."

She shakes her head, and I drop the subject.

"Come out with me," I say without thinking.

She wraps her arms around her shoulders, and I'm afraid that she won't be able to stand on her own two feet much longer, much less come out on a date with me.

"I don't mean as a date. Just that you shouldn't be alone. I can be good, I promise."

She looks down, obviously thinking about it but not yet convinced.

"Just let me feed you and distract you for a few hours. You can talk to me about your grandmother or not. Or you can yell at me and call me names if it will make you feel better. Whatever you need. Today, I'll just be a friend."

"And tomorrow?"

"Tomorrow, I'll go back to being the monster you think I am."

At that comment, I get the tiniest smile out of her.

"I know you are."

I nod.

"I'll come as long as I can leave when I want."

"I'll bring you back whenever you want."

"Yes then."

We both smile when she says yes instead of her giving a less convincing answer.

"Let me just grab my purse."

"No. Change into something comfortable and at least bring your swimsuit."

She frowns. "Why?"

"Because the ocean can be an incredibly healing thing whether I'm there to enjoy it with you or not." I take a breath. "And, if nothing else, I'll get to see you in a bikini."

I wink, and to my surprise, she chuckles. It's not a full-body laugh, but it's enough for now.

"Fine. I'll wear my bikini underneath something more comfortable." She starts walking to her bedroom. "I'll be right back. Make yourself comfortable."

She closes the door to her bedroom and leaves me in her living room. I walk around, staring at all the things in her living room that are varying shades of white. I'm surprised that I don't find many photos in her living room. I don't see any of Wes. The only one I see is a picture of Sloane with who I assume is her grandmother.

I pick the picture up and study it a moment. Sloane is a little younger-looking in the picture but not much younger. She has her arm wrapped around her grandmother's shoulders while her grandmother blows out the candles on her birthday cake. It's a sweet picture. Full of love. It's obvious that Sloane loved her grandmother.

I place the frame back on the end table where I found it, and a familiar feeling washes over me. I shake it off because the feeling makes no sense. I haven't been in this building before and certainly not in Sloane's place.

I walk over to the kitchen counter and see a pile of pictures and papers piled up. I don't think anything of it at first until I spot a surfboard that is very familiar, sticking out from beneath one of the papers. I pull it out and see a picture of myself staring back at me.

What the fuck?

Why does Sloane have a picture of me?

I rifle through more of the pictures. They're all of me. Then, I realize what the pictures are when I spot Wes in the background. Sloane is the one who hired me to take the ad photos and video. That just leaves me even more confused. I know Sloane works for a nonprofit, so why would she want to have photos of a surfer for advertising? It doesn't make sense to me.

"I didn't realize it was you that I had booked; otherwise, I wouldn't have booked you," Sloane says from behind me.

I turn and look at her, and I completely forget about the photographs. "You're beautiful."

She shakes her head and blushes a little, which makes her all the more enduring. She doesn't blush when she should be embarrassed, but one tiny compliment, and she's a blushing fool.

Sloane runs her hand through her hair, shaking out the curls that were there before. "No, I'm not. I'm in a T-shirt and shorts. I don't have an ounce of makeup on, and I'm blotchy from crying. It's not possible to look beautiful at the moment."

I frown, trying to come up with the words that will make her see what I see. I doubt I can convince her of anything in the moment. "It doesn't matter if you believe me or not. You're the most fucking beautiful woman I've ever seen. And, right now, you are more beautiful than I have ever seen you," I say, meaning every fucking word, my eyes glued to hers.

She stares back at me until she is finally convinced that I am telling the truth. I don't know when she'll realize that I never lie. Never. I don't lie to women to get them to leave their husbands. I want an honest fight. I just usually win, which must mean that the women don't really want to get married. Marriage is a ridiculous concept anyway. No one should be with just one person for the rest of their life. People are constantly changing and not always in the same way.

Why would you stay with the same person when you no longer fit together anymore?

I try to search her eyes to see if she is just like the rest of the women, who were looking for an escape from a marriage that they thought would be everything they'd ever dreamed up but realized too late that it was going to be a nightmare that there was no way out of. But whatever she feels, she hides it well. She might just be the exception. She might really love Wes and want to marry him. I just can't see how a woman like her, who seems to have such ambition and is constantly changing and wanting more out of life, would be happy with settling down with one man for the rest of her life.

"The video and pictures we took are for an ad my new head of marketing came up with. I don't love the idea, but she is insistent that, since I spend so much time in Hawaii and many of our donors live or at least vacation here, we need to add more inspiring images of what our children and families could eventually achieve with the money they are given instead of just images of hungry children."

"Why don't you use images of people who have gone through your program and made something of their lives?"

"We did."

"I didn't do any ads with children that have gone through your program.

She shakes her head. "You did."

I pause for a second. "Wes? Really? But he always seems like —" I stop myself from saying how I really feel about Wes.

Sloane smiles though. "Like a spoiled rich kid."

I nod.

"He thinks he needs to act that way to fit in with me and my family."

I glance around her expensive apartment and raise an eyebrow. "I can understand why."

She lets out a huff of air. "I guess so."

I don't want to spend the rest of the evening talking about Wes. My job today is to cheer her up and be her friend. I made a promise, and I won't go back on my promise.

I hold out my arm to her, like the gentleman that I am. "Hungry, or should I take you to the beach first?"

Sloane walks toward me. Her hips sway as she does, and I

have never wished I were standing behind a woman like I do right now.

I think she is going to take my arm, but she stops short.

"Beach. I don't have an appetite for food."

She walks past me and toward the door, and I finally get the view that I was desperate for a second earlier. Her tight ass moves from side to side, just barely covered in her tiny shorts, making the fact that she isn't holding on to my arm so that I could feel her skin worth it.

"You coming, or do I have to go myself?"

I grin. "Definitely coming."

Sloane is beyond independent. She doesn't let me do anything for her as we make our way out of her condo building. I don't get to open a door or press an elevator button or rest my hand on the small of her back to guide her. She avoids me at every turn.

Her surfboard is waiting for her in the lobby when we get down. How they managed to get it so quickly, I have no idea since she just texted them that she needed it when we got into the elevator. But, somehow, they managed or knew that she would need it. Because here it sits.

I run forward to take it off their hands before Sloane is able to.

"Relax, Asher. I appreciate the help, but I can carry my own surfboard."

I hold it up high over my head, so she can't reach it. "I don't care if you can. You shouldn't have to."

She frowns and crosses her arms. "I don't need a man to take care of me. If you think that's why I'm marrying Wes, you're wrong."

"I realize you don't need a man or anyone else to do anything for you. But that doesn't mean you should stop every man from doing something nice for you."

She rolls her eyes and then begins walking toward the parking lot. I can't tear my eyes away from her ass as she walks. I'm too focused on Sloane to notice another woman in the room, one that I should have been paying attention to.

I feel the slap before I notice the girl. I grab my stinging cheek as I look at the woman who just slapped me.

"You're an asshole! I can't believe you had the nerve to come back here. Leave me the fuck alone!" she screams at me before turning and walking out of the condo.

I glance up at Sloane, who has her head cocked to one side, her arms folded across her chest, and the cutest grin ever on her face.

"Who was that?"

"Nicole," I say, realizing why I had a familiar feeling while I was in Sloane's condo. I've been here before—with Nicole.

"And why did she slap you?"

"Because I'm an asshole."

Sloane laughs.

"Did you bring your surfboard? If so, we can just surf right out here. It's a private beach."

"No, I didn't bring it." I think that is the first time I have ever spoken such a sentence. I always bring my surfboard. This is exactly why I always bring my surfboard and swim trunks with me.

"My car is just over this way. I can drive you to wherever you want to grab yours."

I smile when she mentions her car. Of course she wants to drive. She wants to do everything herself. And, since I'm trying to appease her and make her forget about how sad she really is, I'm not going to argue, no matter how much I want to show her how well I could take care of her if she let me.

I follow her to her pristine white Jeep that doesn't look like it has ever been driven.

"Is there something wrong?" Sloane asks when I stop and stare at it.

This woman is the epitome of contradiction. She works for a nonprofit, giving money to those who need it most, but also has more money and spends it like she enjoys showing off the money she has. She likes surfing and adventure but dresses like she never leaves the business room. I can't understand her.

"Nothing," I say.

I place her surfboard on top of her Jeep, quickly strapping it in, before climbing into the passenger side. Sloane is already on the driver's side and begins backing out as soon as I get in.

We drive in silence. It's clear that Sloane is lost in thoughts of her grandmother, bringing back the feelings of sadness and pain that I can't stand to watch. It's not hot in her Jeep. The AC works almost too well, which is strange for me since I can't recall my truck's AC ever working.

I roll my window down and stick my hand out into the warm breeze, like you should in Hawaii.

"What are you doing?" she asks sternly.

"Enjoying Hawaii."

Her hair blows as the breeze gets stronger inside the car. She runs her hand through her hair, trying to keep the wind from further tangling it.

"But it's too warm outside, and the AC is working fine. Why would I open the window?"

I laugh and shake my head. "Do you really never drive around with the windows open?"

"No. It's much too warm here."

"Turn the AC off, and open your window."

"No."

"Stop being stubborn, and just do it."

She looks at me like I'm mad but finally concedes. Her hair becomes even more tangled, blowing in front of her face as she drives. She seems agitated and annoyed, which is the opposite of what I'm going for.

"Now, relax, and stick your hand out the window."

She raises an eyebrow at me.

I laugh, my whole body shaking. I can't help it.

"Are you sure you grew up here? You are acting like you grew up in outer space."

She frowns, clearly not amused.

"Like this," I say, sticking my hand out the window.

She does the same, and it only takes seconds for her to relax. To breathe and become one with the wind, letting go of some of the sadness was overtaking her. But there is too much sadness and pain in her for a simple car ride with the wind blowing around us to fix. Not that anything is going to fix the pain or sadness. I know that as well as anyone. I've experienced it myself and caused it in others. I've watched them all handle the pain in different ways. Some handle it better than others, but then some weren't really in love.

Sloane loved her grandmother. So, the pain will never go away. But she does need to learn to live with it, and the sooner she does, the better. If only for my selfish reasons. Because, the sooner she heals, the sooner I can rip her heart out.

"Pull over," I say.

"Why?" Sloane asks but doesn't pull over.

"For once, can you just do what I tell you without asking why?"

She frowns. "No. We haven't known each other long enough for me to do that."

I laugh. "Do you do what Wes tells you without asking why?"

She scrunches her nose. "No."

"Exactly. It doesn't matter who is asking. You always have to be in control. For once in your life, let someone else have control. Don't think. Just do."

I reach over and touch her hand that has a firm hold on the steering wheel. She doesn't flinch even though that was what I expected. She doesn't glance down either. She acts like I'm not even touching her.

She's a much better actor than I am. I can feel my heart pounding in my chest at the touch of her soft skin. I have to be good today. I'm used to practicing self-control. But Sloane makes that incredibly hard to do.

"Pull over," I say calmly.

Sloane takes a deep breath. I watch her chest rise and fall and wish she weren't wearing the T-shirt covering the bikini underneath. Better yet, I wish she were wearing nothing.

Sloane pulls the car over onto the side of the road.

"Now, put the car in park."

She does without hesitation.

"Turn the car off."

She slowly reaches up, and I reluctantly move my hand away from hers as she turns the car off.

"Take a deep breath, and then get out of the car."

I watch her chest rise and fall again, and then she gets out of the car. I do the same and pull her surfboard off the top of the car. I begin carrying it to the beach.

"What are we doing? You don't have your surfboard or swim trunks, and this is one of the worst places for surf on the island. There isn't even anyone here."

I shake my head from side to side. "No questions. You have to trust me. This is what you need."

She frowns, but I keep walking toward the edge of the water with her surfboard in tow, not giving her another choice.

She walks behind me.

When I get to the water, I stop and wait for her to catch up. I hand her back her surfboard.

"Now, surf, and don't think. About me or Wes or your grandmother. Or anything else. Just surf. Go through the motions."

She opens her mouth to say something, but I put a finger up to her lips to stop her. Her lips are as soft as I imagined. She bites her lip, and I pull my hand away.

"Don't say anything. Now, go." I point toward the ocean.

She grins. "I was only going to say, can I take my T-shirt and shorts off first?"

I want to say no because it doesn't matter. She's thinking too much, and she needs to just get in the water. But I'm desperate to see her in nothing but her bikini. I can just imagine her walking back toward me after surfing, beads of water dripping down her breasts. I need to see her body like that. Although a white T-shirt drenched in water might be equally as awesome.

"It was implied," I say.

"Sure it was."

She shimmies out of her shorts first, but her T-shirt is long enough that it covers her ass, revealing nothing new to me. But then she removes her shirt, revealing the toned body that she was hiding beneath her T-shirt.

Damn. I don't know what I was expecting, but I wasn't expecting this.

She's toned and fit beneath her tiny black bikini. I can see the muscles rippling in her stomach, arms, and legs. But she also has the perfect amount of curves outlining her muscles. Her breasts have me aching to touch them. Her hips are curvy, making me want to grab her and have her right here in the sand. Even though I've done that before and as much as I like the beach and ocean, fucking a woman on it is much worse than the fantasy.

She doesn't smile as she begins walking into the ocean. Instead, she seems determined. She walks in a ways before she gets on the board and starts paddling out. The waves are pretty tame here, and there isn't anyone out here that she has to pay attention to. No, this is the perfect spot for her to clear her head and get used to the pain she is feeling.

I just wish I had my own board, so I could join her.

It doesn't take her long to paddle out until I can barely make out the curves in her body from where I stand.

She takes her time in choosing a wave. And then she is up on her board, surfing with obvious experience. She doesn't do anything fancy. But the way she moves over the ocean is beautiful. She glides easily, like she has been doing it her whole life. I could watch her for hours.

The wave suddenly changes and causes Sloane to lose her balance and prematurely fall off the board. The wave crashes down on top of her with a lot of force. I know it's not enough to keep her down for long. I know the wave wasn't that bad. But, still, I can't help but throw off my shirt, jump into the water, and swim out to her to ensure that she makes it out of the water. To air. To safety.

I swim as fast and as hard as I can to reach her. I try to calm my beating heart and nerves that are shooting through my body. I don't understand the feeling. I don't understand why I care so much if she is alive or dead. In pain or not. She is nothing to me.

Still, I swim hard, not thinking about why my heart is beating hard in my chest. Or why I care if something happens to her. I dive under the water, swimming faster until I see her body right in front of me. I grab hold of her and look up to see the wave has stopped pounding down on top of us. And then I kick hard over and over until we reach the top.

We each take a breath of air at the same time when our heads hit the surface. Sloane flips her head back to get her hair out of her face, and she scowls at me. Her eyes look unforgiving, a deep V has formed between her eyes, and her mouth turns down into more than a frown.

"What are you doing?"

"Saving you. You went down and didn't come back up for air for quite a while. I wanted to make sure you didn't die."

She shakes her head as she wades in the water and rests her arms on her surfboard. "I don't need saving or rescuing. I have surfed before even if I am a bit rusty."

"I know."

"Then, why are you here?"

"Because I can't help but be near you."

"I thought you weren't going to hit on me today."

"I'm not. I'm just telling you the truth since you are so insistent on asking a million questions, needing to know everything."

She doesn't say anything else, but I can tell she is deep in thought again, no longer here with me.

"Swim back out, and go again," I say.

She turns to do just that. At least, now, she is listening to me instead of questioning. She pauses though after swimming a foot or so and faces me.

"What are you going to do?"

"Join you."

"How? You don't have your surfboard."

I grin. "Sure I do."

I start swimming out while she paddles on her surfboard. When she stops, I swim up behind her, guiding her toward the front of the surfboard while I climb on behind her. Neither of us says anything, and I have honestly never surfed with someone else on the same board before. But it can't be that hard. She's more than capable on a surfboard, and I'll figure out the rest, no problem.

We wait through the first wave, agreeing it's not the right one without having to say anything to each other.

When the next wave comes, I say, "Start paddling."

We both do.

"Stand up," I say after a few seconds of paddling.

Sloane does, and I do a second later. Then, we are both up on the board at the same time. I take a step forward and place my hands on her hips as I begin maneuvering the board through the wave. She moves with me as I move us as one. It feels different, maneuvering while having to think about someone else on the board. I can't just do what I want. I have to ensure that she wants to go the same way as me. I have to think about her, too.

I want to show her what a surfboard can really do though, so I grip her hips harder and begin moving us higher onto the wave. She doesn't question me. She goes with me. We surf until the wave takes us close to shore. We step off at the same time, both speechless.

Our eyes lock after such an intimate moment together. I don't know what I see in her eyes. I'm used to being able to read people, but I can't read her. She doesn't give anything away with her eyes. I just know what I hope I'm seeing there. I hope it's the same thing that I'm feeling.

I reach my hand up to her cheek. "I want to kiss you," I say.

I wait for her to slap me. A slap always follows when I say something so bold. I brace for it. But it never comes. Instead, she leans in closer to me, like she is considering it. Like she is desperate for it. I feel her warm breath against my lips. I have to ball my hands into fists to keep from closing in the last few inches and kissing her.

I won't kiss her though. If she cheats on Wes, it has to be her choice. That's the only way to steal her heart, to ensure she's mine, and then I'll toss her aside when I'm through with her. She has to be the one who does the betrayal.

When she realizes that no temptation is going to get me to be the one to make the first move, she steps back and turns to look out over the ocean at the sun that is just now beginning to set over the ocean.

"We should go sit on the beach and watch the sunset, so we can try to dry off before getting back into my car. We forgot to bring towels," Sloane says so matter-of-factly. Like the almost kiss didn't happen. Like I haven't affected her at all.

My eyes widen as I stare at her walking back toward the shore. I begin to follow her. I walk until I'm standing right next to her on the beach. She's staring at the sunset while I'm gaping at her.

"What are you doing?" she asks, still staring straight ahead at the sunset, while she wrings out her wet hair.

"Gaping at how you never cease to surprise me."

"Why is that?"

"You never behave in the way that I think you will."

She nods. "Would it surprise you to hear that you aren't the first person to make that observation?"

I laugh. "No, I guess it wouldn't."

She looks at me. "I get it from my grandmother. My unpredictability."

I walk over and find my T-shirt that I threw on the beach before I jumped into the water. I pick it up and carry it over to where Sloane is standing on the beach, trying to dry off. I lay it on the ground.

"Here, sit on the T-shirt, so you don't get sand all over you."

She sits on my T-shirt, and I sit on the sand next to her.

Sloane laughs at me.

I rub my neck as I listen to her beautiful laugh that I didn't think I would get to hear today. "You're going to have to tell me what is so funny."

She keeps laughing though until her whole body is rocking

back and forth from the force of her laughter. "I'm sorry," she says in between laughs. "It's really not funny. I don't understand why I'm laughing at all. It's just that you thought I should sit on your T-shirt to avoid getting sand on me, but then you sat down on the sand. And, unless you are walking home, you are going to get sand in my car."

I stare at her, taking in her laugh again that continues to force itself out of her. But she has a point. So, I get up and rinse myself off in the water. And then I march back to her.

"What are you doing?" she asks, still laughing.

I don't respond to her basically never-ending question. I guess I should dictate everything that I am doing, as I'm doing it to satisfy her. She really is a control freak.

I plop down behind her so that I can sit on the tiny bit of remaining T-shirt that she is not sitting on. She squeals and laughs, like she probably would if Wes had sat down behind her.

"You're getting me all wet," she squeals as the water drips off my chest and onto her back.

"Damn it! I promised I wouldn't hit on you; otherwise, I would have a great line about getting you wet."

This causes her to laugh hysterically all over again. She throws her head back, hitting me square in the jaw.

"Oh my God! I'm sorry," she says, still laughing.

I laugh now. "I don't think you are the least bit sorry. You probably think I deserved it."

"You're right. I'm not sorry at all. You deserved that and more."

Sloane continues to laugh until her laugh turns into hiccups. I rub her back under the guise of trying to calm her down and make the hiccups go away, but I also can't stand to be this close to her and not touch any part of her body, except for our legs that are barely touching. Her skin is soft and warm.

"The sunset is beautiful," she says as she leans back a little but not enough so that she is leaning against my chest, like I want.

"You're beautiful," I say automatically.

"That sounds like you are hitting on me."

"Nope. Just stating a fact."

She takes a deep breath. I can tell from watching her rib cage rising and falling.

"Thank you for this," she says.

I don't say anything because the hesitation in her voice tells me she needs to say more.

"I needed this. I don't know how you knew this was what I'd need, but I did. I wouldn't have survived being alone tonight."

I think she's crying, but I can't be sure. But, from the sniffling sound in her voice, I can guess.

I don't comfort her though. She doesn't need that. She needs to find her way on her own.

"I don't know why I feel her loss so much. She hasn't been in my life in the last five years. Not really. She had Alzheimer's, and she lived in a nursing home. I tried to visit as often as I could, but she didn't know who I was. She's been gone for the last five years. I thought I'd come to terms with the fact that the woman who had raised me was gone."

She turns and faces me, and I see the full tears coming down her face.

"She's really gone now though. Body and mind. She was the only person who ever really made me feel loved." Her voice is shaky.

I know that there are no words to make it better for her. I can't help her through this. She has to deal with this pain, this sadness, this new reality. All I can do is wrap my arms around her and let her know that she isn't alone.

So, that is exactly what I do.

She resists me at first, pushing my arms away, but I hold on tighter. Not because I'm hitting on her or because I need to feel her close to me. But because I know she needs the connection to another human being right now.

She finally relaxes against my chest, as I continue to hold her in my arms. She continues to cry as we both look out over the ocean as the sun sets. We don't say anything else. Sloane can't get any other words out between her tears anyway. And I can't say anything that will make her stop crying. So, we just sit until the warmth of the sun is long gone, and there is nothing but the noise of the highway behind us and the ocean waves in front of us.

"Do you want me to take you home now?" I whisper in her ear.

She doesn't answer. I move my head forward, so it is closer to her face that is lying against my chest, and I listen to her calm breathing. She's asleep.

I'll have to find a way to get her back to her condo at some point. But, for now, I just want to sit here, in one of my favorite places, holding a beautiful woman who I don't think, no matter how hard I try, I will fully understand.

I think about the last words she said to me.

"She was the only person who ever really made me feel loved."

I don't know if her words were true or if she was just upset and said it because she was missing Wes and not feeling loved. But I have to find out. Because I can't really steal her from Wes if he's never really loved her.

CHAPTER

TEN

Asher

I carried Sloane back to her car that night. She didn't wake up. She didn't stir. She was too exhausted from dealing with her grief to wake up.

I drove her back to my place after I realized I would never get her back into her place without waking her. I figured, after she slept for an hour or so, she would wake up, and then she could drive herself back home in her car.

She never woke up though.

I placed her in my bed and fell asleep on the couch, waiting for her to wake up.

The next morning, she was gone without a word, which didn't surprise me. What did was how early in the morning she'd left. I'm always awake before the sun. She woke up and left before I did.

I haven't spoken to or seen her in almost two months. The wedding was postponed after her grandmother's death to give her time to mourn, to heal. I've been busy with winning a couple of surfing competitions. There haven't been any wedding-related

85

events that I've had to attend. But that's not why I have stayed away. I've stayed away because I'm torn.

Sloane doesn't make anything clear. I can't read if she really loves Wes or not. And, since I can't tell how she feels, I don't know how I want to pursue her or if I want to pursue her at all. Not because I've had a change of heart. I still want to destroy her. I still want to steal her heart. I just need to give her time to realign her loyalty to Wes because, after that night, I know I could have had her in my bed. I laugh because I did have her in my bed. But she would have fucked me that morning if she had stayed. That is why I suspect she left before I woke up.

I also know the longer that I stay away, the more she will think about me. The more she will build up that night in her head as being either one of the most meaningful moments in her life or something that makes her hate me even more. Either way, when I walk into the church and see her again, her emotions will be amplified, which will make them much easier for me to read. The only problem with my plan is that my ability to control myself is dwindling. I want Sloane more than ever, and even if it's not the right time to steal her heart, I'm not sure I'm going to be able to resist her.

I get out of my pickup truck and walk toward the beautiful stone cathedral where the rehearsal dinner is to be held, and the rehearsal is to take place on the beach just outside the building. It's a beautiful building, but it is nothing compared to the beach.

If I were getting married, I would do it on the beach with as few people as possible. I laugh. Not that I would ever get married. But, from the number of cars parked in the parking lot just for the rehearsal, I know that this wedding is going to be a big affair.

I enter the church and immediately feel everyone's eyes turn to me. I look down at how I'm dressed in the same shorts and button-down shirt that I wore the last time I saw Sloane. I thought I was dressed up enough for a rehearsal. I was wrong.

I glance around the room at the suits and formal dresses that everyone else is wearing. But I don't apologize for wearing something casual. I'm not going to bother spending money on something that I'd wear once and then never wear again.

"You made it," Wes says to me, holding out his fist that I bump against mine.

"Of course, man. This seems like quite the ordeal here," I say.

Wes smiles. "Yep. This is heaven to me. Everyone that I care about is here, and tomorrow, I'll get to marry this amazing woman," Wes says while wrapping his arm around Sloane's waist.

She smiles at me while holding on to him. I hate watching her with him. I hate it. But, other than picking her up, carrying her over my shoulder, and literally kidnapping her, I don't really have a choice at the moment.

"It's good to see you again, Sloane. Excited to get married tomorrow?" I ask.

She stands in front of Wes, and he possessively puts his arms around her, which seems strange for her to allow when she is such an independent person.

"Of course she's excited. Aren't you, honey?" Wes asks.

Sloane nods, her smile never faltering. She looks like a happy bride on the brink of marital bliss as she stands in the arms of her fiancé in a white lace dress that makes her boobs look amazing and her legs long and lean. But she's not happy. I know her well enough to know that, no matter how much she loves Wes, she's not happy with him, and she won't be happy marrying him.

She's made my decision for me. I must steal her before she gets married tomorrow. I'll actually be doing her a service. She'll have to deal with the pain for a couple of days to avoid a lifetime of unhappiness.

"I'm sure she is," I say, sticking my hands in my pockets to keep myself from ripping Sloane out of Wes's arms.

The minister begins waving Sloane and Wes toward the front of the church.

"I guess that's our cue to go," Wes says, grabbing hold of Sloane's hand and leading her to the front of the church where the minister stands.

I follow slowly behind, keeping my hands in my pockets and staying on the outskirts of the crowd that is gathering around the couple.

"I'm Dean, the minister who will be conducting the ceremony tomorrow. Tonight, we are just going to run through the rehearsal, so everyone knows what they will be doing tomorrow. Then, you will be able to enjoy the dinner that the bride and groom are providing you.

"There has been a change of plans due to the weather tomorrow. Due to the extreme heat, we will be having the ceremony as well as the reception inside the church."

My eyes go to Sloane. She doesn't give away any hint of sadness. Or at least she doesn't think she is giving away any hint that she doesn't want to get married inside this damn church instead of out on the beach. But the people who know her well or take the time to know her at all can tell. I can tell even if there wasn't the tiniest bit of welling in her eyes. I can tell that this isn't what she wants.

The minister continues to talk about how the rehearsal is going to happen and what everybody needs to be doing, but I don't listen. All I can see is Sloane. How she kisses Wes. How she mirrors his movements. How she is anything but independent when he's around. It's bizarre—her behavior.

People start moving into positions, and I follow Wes to the

side of the church. Wes says something to me and his other two groomsmen standing behind me. I nod automatically and then follow Wes when he walks out into position. I stand next to him with the other groomsmen standing behind me. We all know where to stand, despite none of us listening.

Music starts up, and the bridesmaids begin walking toward us. It seems to take forever to get them down the aisle even though there are only three of them. Then, they stand opposite us. All beautiful, of course, but none beautiful enough to make me give up my plan to steal Sloane. She is my only focus.

The music changes, and Sloane finally starts walking down the aisle. She's beautiful, of course, as she walks down the aisle by herself. Her blonde hair seems to blow, as if a fan were directed on her the whole time she walks. Her skin seems to glow. Her eyes though are what interest me the most. Everyone else who sees her walking down the aisle assumes she is looking at Wes, holding his gaze.

She isn't though. Her gaze is on me.

Sloane looks at me the whole time she walks down the aisle, and her eyes tell me everything. That she wants me to rescue her. To save her from this. I grin because that is exactly what I'm going to do.

Sloane makes it down the aisle and goes through the motions of the ceremony as the minister explains everything that is going to happen. And then he calls for everyone to do everything again. Everyone sighs and moans quietly to themselves. With large fake smiles on our faces, we all go through the motions again while being completely bored out of our minds.

The only positive thing I get out of it is being able to study Sloane as she walks. Every curve of her gorgeous tan skin. Every curl of her blonde hair. The green color of her eyes. The confidence in which she walks or does anything.

The minister finally dismisses us, saying that we can all head into the dining hall where we can enjoy a dinner on the bride and groom. I head into the dining hall with the other grooms-men. I take a seat at the same table as they do even though I know they all want to punch me in the face. I've learned though not to take it personally. It is just the reaction I provoke in people.

Waiters start bringing out the first course of soup and salad. But the happy couple still hasn't made their appearance. I pick at the salad. I've never been one for eating anything remotely healthy.

The waiters take the first course away and start serving the main course of chicken and vegetables. I scan the room but still don't see where the bride- and groom-to-be are. A few other people have noticed, too. I can see the worry and anxiety on some of their faces.

I get up from the table and hear a woman say to her husband, "It's strange that the bride and groom haven't made it to the rehearsal dinner yet."

The husband laughs. "They are probably just doing it in a back room somewhere."

I feel a tightness in my chest as I think about that possibility. It's never bothered me before when the women I was trying to steal slept with their fiancés. But knowing that is what Sloane could be doing drives me crazy. I don't want Wes touching her or kissing her or fucking her. I don't want him anywhere near her. She's mine.

I start walking back to the chapel where the rehearsals took place, as it was the last place that I saw either of them. The second I enter the chapel, I hear their voices ringing throughout the room. I'm surprised that we couldn't hear them arguing from the dining room just down the hallway from here.

"No, we aren't postponing until the weather cooperates so that we can get married outside!" Wes shouts.

"But it's important to me!" Sloane shouts back.

"Isn't being married more important than where we get married?" Wes shouts.

"Of course, but this is the one thing I care about. The beach reminds me of my grandmother, which is why I want to get married there instead of in this church."

I slowly walk up, trying not to be noticed, but they both seem so entranced in their arguing that I don't think they would notice me, no matter how loud I was being. They start walking, and I keep following. Sloane starts running out of the church, visibly upset and shaking with anger.

"I'm so tired of hearing about your grandmother. We postponed the wedding in the first place because of your grandmother's death. I don't think we have to do everything because of your goddamn grandmother."

Tears well in Sloane's eyes, and I can't stand it any longer.

I start to move forward when Sloane says, "I can't breathe."

"Sure you can. You just don't want to admit that you're wrong, and I'm right."

But Sloane truly can't breathe. Her face is turning bright red, and she falls back to the ground. I run forward at the same time that Wes does. Her face has started to swell.

"Sloane, what's wrong?" I ask.

But she can't answer me. I can tell she is running out of oxygen fast. I pinch her nose and lower my mouth to hers, breathing a breath into her, but the air barely seems to make a difference.

I feel something sharp hit my neck, followed by a buzzing sound. Bees. She must be allergic. I grab her purse that is lying next to her.

"Call 911, Wes," I say as I dig through it and find the EpiPen that is inside.

I quickly read through the instructions, but I know I'm

running out of time. So, I remove the cap and then jab it into her thigh, like the instructions say.

"Come on, Sloane, breathe. You're going to be fine. Just relax, and try to breathe."

She slowly takes a breath and starts to sit up. My heart slows when I see that she is going to make it.

"Thank you," she whispers.

I nod, but saving her did nothing to stop my own anger. If anything, it just made me angrier. I help Sloane to her feet and then over to a bench outside the church where she can wait for the ambulance to come and check her over. And then I turn toward Wes, who is standing next to the bench, and I punch him square in the face. He completely falls back, startled by my punch.

"You don't deserve a woman like Sloane," I say, staring at Wes now lying on the floor, still in complete shock.

I turn to face Sloane as the ambulance pulls up. "Don't marry him. Not because I want you and am desperate to claim you, to fuck you, but because you deserve better than an asshole dick of a man who doesn't understand how important your grandmother is to you. You don't have to choose me, but don't choose him either. You deserve love, not years of unhappiness."

ELEVEN

Asher

I grab the six-pack of beer and take it out to the beach. I considered just going home after I punched Wes. I left the rehearsal before Wes came to his senses and decided to start a fight. But I stuck around in the parking lot long enough to see that Sloane didn't even have to go to the hospital. They checked her over and determined that the EpiPen was enough. That she was going to be okay. She went back into the rehearsal, and I left. I couldn't bear to stay and watch her prepare to marry him.

My surfboard is in the back of my truck. I consider bringing it down to the beach with me, but I don't really feel like surfing. Instead, I plop down on the sand with my beer.

I'll drink for a while, maybe take a dip in the ocean, and then sleep off the alcohol in the back of my truck or here on the beach. I open the first beer, trying to do anything but think about Wes and Sloane. I've never punched anyone before. I know that punching someone accomplishes nothing but making the puncher feel a bit better—at least, for a moment. But, now that I have, I want to go back and beat the shit out of Wes for treating Sloane so poorly.

And Sloane...I have no idea what she is going to do. Marry him most likely. I don't see her canceling the wedding the night before. She's different than all the other women I've seduced. She is stronger and no-nonsense, all business. I'm not even sure that she is marrying Wes because she loves him. There has to be another reason that I am overlooking. Something that makes her feel like she has to go through with it—not because she loves him, but because that is what is best for her future.

Maybe her company's future? I have no idea.

But Sloane was right about one thing. I was going to lose this game. I was never going to claim her. Even if she decides not to marry Wes, she will never be mine. She is too intelligent, too independent, too rational to let her heart go to a man like me.

I sip on my beer, trying to forget about all of it. I stare out at the ocean. I should take a trip somewhere. Get away from my normal life for a week or two. I've always wanted to travel overseas. But it would have to be somewhere without a beach because, after our time together on the beach, in the ocean, I can't be out here without thinking of her.

It was a mistake, coming here now. I should have just gone back to my shack. Maybe then I can forget about her. I glance down at the six-pack on my left. Maybe, after drinking all of them, I will forget about her.

"Can I join you?" a soft voice says behind me.

I freeze, not sure if she is really here or if I am imagining her.

She doesn't wait for me to answer. Sloane just sits down in the sand next to me, not caring that her white dress is going to be covered in sand. She takes a beer and opens the cap with the bottom of her shoe. She didn't bother asking if she could have one. She isn't that kind of girl. She doesn't ask permission for anything; she just does.

"Thank you," she says after a long pause.

I stare at her with wide eyes. I'm not sure if anyone has ever thanked me before, for anything. And I never expected to get multiple thank-yous from her, of all people.

"You really need to stop thanking me. For however bad Wes treats you, I'm worse."

She sips her beer. I watch her mouth close around it, and I can't help but imagine her lips wrapped around my cock. Although I don't see that happening—ever.

"I'm not getting married tomorrow," she says.

I nod. "I guessed that. I'm not sorry. I don't think he's good enough for you."

She finishes her beer. "I'm not sorry either. Not really."

She takes another beer out, which makes me smile at her.

I finish my own beer and start on a second. "So, what now?"

"First, I'm going to finish the rest of these beers with you."

I grin. "Of course. And then?"

"And then you are going to fuck me and make me forget about Wes."

I spew the beer out of my mouth. She looks at me straight-faced though, and I know she is dead serious.

"You surprise the hell out of me, Sloane."

She drinks down half of her second beer. "You don't surprise me at all."

"I'm not sure if that was meant as a compliment or a dis, but I'll take it if it means I get to fuck you."

"I don't like surprises."

"I love surprises if they come from you."

Her lips crash with mine, surprising the hell out of me again. Her kiss is hungry, like she is desperate for more and more and more. And I'm more than happy to give her everything she wants and more.

I kiss her back, equally as hungry. My tongue slides into her mouth, and to my surprise, she lets me. Each step I take with her is going to surprise me because I thought she hated me.

She has every reason to. I broke up her wedding. I ruined her life.

But she is kissing me like I'm the only man she has ever wanted. My hand tangles in her hair, pulling her closer to me, and at the same time, she pushes herself on top of me. We fall back and break our kiss.

Sloane lies on top of me, breathing heavily from our quick make-out session. We stare at each other for a moment, deciding if we want this to go any further.

"We can stop. No one has to know that you kissed me. You could still go back to Wes. But, if you do this, he will never take you back," I warn.

I've seen it before, and as much as I thought I wanted to destroy her, I was wrong. I don't want to hurt her. I care too much about her, which is strange, especially since I have never slept with her.

"Don't ever stop. I need this. I don't want Wes. I want you even if only for one night."

I pull her bottom lip into my mouth, bringing her lips back to mine. Her hands go back around my neck, and my hands rub against her bare back, running over her smooth skin, as we kiss. Each kiss, our tongues dive deeper into each other's mouth, showing how desperate we are for each other.

Without thinking, I begin to undo the zipper that starts around her waist. I slowly unzip it until my hand can slip beneath the lace fabric. My hand slides over her ass, and I find the same lace material covering it.

Sloane starts tugging at my shirt, running her hand over my abs and up my chest. I love the feel of her soft hands so firm against me, demanding what she wants. I've never had a woman so clearly tell me what she wants without even saying a word.

She wants me to take her here, on the beach.

The wind picks up, and salt water and sand brush over us. And I'm reminded why I never fuck women on the beach.

"My car is"—I kiss her soft, luscious lips—"just"—she kisses me, stopping me from speaking—"over—"

Sloane shuts me up again with her kisses. I don't give a fuck that rough seashells are poking into my ass as she rides me. I don't care that we are going to get salt water in our eyes as I fuck her. I won't be able to close my eyes for a second because I would hate to miss even a moment with her. I don't give a shit that I'm going to find sand for days to come in places that I don't even want to think about.

I'm going to fuck her here, on the beach, where anyone could see us, because I can't help but give her everything she wants and give myself exactly what I want as well. Because I've never wanted anything more than this completely unpredictable, self-sufficient, beautiful woman.

"I want to strip you naked, but I couldn't stand it if anyone else got to see you naked on the beach," I say.

She lifts up the hem of her dress and jerks it over her head, revealing her black lace bra and underwear that she somehow hid under the white material of her dress, like the devil she hides underneath her angel facade. My eyes widen from the shock of what she just did and how perfect her body is. How her breasts overflow from her bra, begging me to touch them.

"No one comes to this beach. And it doesn't matter if anyone does. I'm not going to last long enough for them to get much of a show anyway."

She kisses me again, and I forget that we are on a public beach and that anyone could see her. I no longer fucking care.

"Plus, I'm not ashamed of my body. I know I look hot, naked or not."

I bite her bottom lip again. "I couldn't agree more."

She grabs my dick from beneath my shorts and underwear,

and I cry out like a fucking girl. I didn't even realize she had found a way through the fabric of my shorts. Her kisses and body are so fucking fantastic that I can't even realize anything else that is going on in the world. I blame it on the fact that all my blood is now pooled in my dick instead of my brain.

Still, I can't have her completely exposed if someone decides to come looking. So, I roll us over in the sand until she's on the bottom, and I'm on top.

"Can't handle a woman in control?" she asks, her eyes full of lust and her lips plump from all the kissing.

I chuckle. "Oh, I would love to see you take control and ride me. I don't think there is anything I want more. But there is no way I'm letting anyone have a chance at seeing you naked. I want to be the only one. I'm too controlling about things that are *mine*."

"I don't like to be claimed. I'm not anyone's."

I roughly kiss her until she is purring a little bit in her throat. And, when I stop, she has a blank look on her face, which makes my grin wider.

"Well, I'm very much up to the challenge of making you mine."

I kiss her again as she pushes down my shorts when I realize...

"Shit."

"What?" She curiously looks at me and then around the beach, assuming I spotted someone looking at us.

As I look at her, I scowl at my unpreparedness. "I don't have a condom."

She grins and then lets out a small chuckle before reaching into her bra and pulling out a gold little square that contains a condom.

"Thank God," I say, grabbing it from her and ripping it open.

I don't waste time in thinking about why she had a condom

in her bra, if she was planning on using it with Wes. I roll it on my dick before sliding my fingers under her panties. I feel the moisture, that I caused, immediately cover my fingers as I find her entrance and slip them between her folds. She moans, and it is a beautiful sound that I never thought I would hear.

I spread the liquid up over her clit, and she bites my lip to keep from screaming. As it is, her screams are loud enough that I'm sure everyone within a square mile can hear her.

"Fuck me, Asher. Make me belong to you."

I slip inside her, and it's heaven.

"I'm never leaving again," I groan as I move inside her.

"Fuck, I don't want you to stop—ever."

I fuck her against the sand as the waves crash against us. I thought I was in love with the ocean and beach before, but now, I know I will never get enough of it. Not after I've had her here.

I thrust and move and build us both until neither of us can hold out any longer, no matter how desperate we are to make this moment last forever.

"Jesus Christ, Asher!" Sloane cries as she comes.

And I come right along with her.

I collapse on top of Sloane, feeling every inch of our bodies pressed together. "You're mine now," I say. I don't add forever. Despite how much I want this to be forever.

Jesus Christ! What the hell is wrong with me? I can't want her forever.

We both hear the sirens in the distance at the same time. I jump off of her and grab her hand, pulling her up and holding her close to me, like I'm going to be able to protect her against the police.

Not likely.

I scoop up her dress off the sand and hand it to her. I pull up my pants and grab my shirt and beer, and then we both start running toward the parking lot.

I don't know why we are both running like the police are going to come arrest us. From a distance, we look plenty clothed for the beach. She's wearing her bra and panties that could easily be mistaken for a bikini, and I'm wearing shorts. But, still, we run like we are running for our lives.

When we get to the parking lot, I don't give her the chance to go back to her car. Actually, I don't even see her car in the parking lot. Instead, I pull her straight to my truck. I open the passenger door and help her inside before running around to the driver's side and jumping in. I turn the key to start the truck up, but of course, it doesn't start.

"Shit," I curse.

I jump out of the car and bang the top of the hood. It still doesn't start.

"Shit, shit, shit."

Sloane rolls down the window. "It sounds like a problem with the starter. Have you checked the wires?"

I don't question how she knows so much about cars. Of course I've tried it before. I've had plenty of experience with getting cars to start. But I humor her and try it anyway. To my surprise, it starts right up.

I jump back into the truck and peel out of the parking lot. I start heading back toward my shack on the beach just as the sirens begin to get loud enough that I'm sure they are right on top of us. I glance in the rearview mirror and see the police heading into the parking lot we just vacated.

Sloane laughs and exhales at the same time. It's a nervous laugh, more like a release after the tense moment we just had. She begins to put her dress back on and then buckles her seat belt as I drive.

"I'm sure the police weren't after us," she says.

"Maybe," I say, trying not to lie. I'm sure they were after us. Or at least *me*.

"Still, it was exciting nonetheless." She dusts off sand from her body. "I'm going to be getting sand out of places for weeks."

I laugh and relax a little, watching her try to dust off sand out of her hair and body but to no avail.

"It's not funny," she says with a smile. "You should look at yourself. It's going to take you at least as long to get rid of all the sand."

"What makes you think I want to get rid of the sand? I live at the beach, and every time the sand rubs against my skin, I'll have a reminder of how I made you mine, if only for a few minutes on the beach."

She blushes a little, and it's the most adorable thing in the world. I take her hand and hold it, like we have been together forever. Like it's the most normal thing in the world to do. And, to my surprise, she seems to relax.

"Where did you park your car? I can take you back to it if you want or take you home or..."

"I want to stay at your place tonight. I can't face my family at my condo. Or Wes. I think you owe me enough to let me spend one night with you."

I grin. "You're welcome to stay at my place for as long as you like."

What the hell has happened to me? I don't say things like that. I don't let women stay for as long as they want. I call the shots.

"Just remember that my place doesn't have as nice of amenities as you are used to."

She cocks her head to one side. "The shack I stayed in is your only place?"

I nod.

She smiles. "Really? It's your only place? You make who knows how much money with your sponsorships and championship winnings, and you don't have a nicer place than that shack and this beat-up truck that doesn't even run properly."

"Yep."

"Why?"

"Because I have realized that possessions don't make me happy. Even when…"

"Even when what?"

"Nothing. It doesn't matter. I just realized that I was happier in a shack on the beach with awesome sunsets than a large mansion with lots of rooms."

She smiles. "I prefer the mansions."

I laugh. "Well, good thing we aren't getting married then or doing anything beyond tonight. We would make a terrible couple. We have nothing in common."

"You're right. We would be miserable together."

"Yep. Miserable."

I turn left onto the gravel road leading toward my shack. "Last chance. I can always take you to a hotel to stay at tonight if you prefer." Although that is the last fucking thing I want. I want her in my bed, shower, couch. I want to claim her in every inch of my shack if this is our last night together.

"I think I can handle the shack for one night."

I exhale deeply as I relax, knowing that I get to have her at least one more time. Or a dozen times if I get my way tonight.

I pull up next to my shack of a house and turn off the engine. Then, I hop down out of my truck and run over to Sloane's side of the car to open the door, like the gentleman that I am. I hold my hand out to her to help her down. Her dress is still undone, barely hanging on to her body, as she begins walking toward the front door.

"The door is unlocked, so just go on in. I need to get my surfboard out of the truck."

"You don't keep your front door locked?"

"No. Why would I?"

She smiles and then walks into my home. I hurriedly take

my surfboard out of the truck and rest it on the rack to keep it out of the elements in case it rains, as it does so often here in the early summer. And then I run inside to find Sloane.

I open the door and find Sloane already completely naked, standing in my living room/bedroom—depending on how you look at it since I really only have one large room that is everything.

She turns and grins at me before she nibbles on her finger. "Your mouth is hanging open," she says, her smile widening.

I instantly close my mouth. "I'm sorry. You are just so incredible."

My eyes go up and down her body, drinking in every drop of her that I felt beneath me earlier but never got to fully appreciate.

"I was going to shower to get cleaned up, but you don't seem to have a shower or bathroom of any type."

I laugh. "I have a shower and bathroom. It's just outside. But I might demand payment in order for you to use it." I take a step forward.

She grins widely and cocks her head to one side. "And if I don't want to give you payment?"

"Then, I guess you are going to have to stay dirty."

She bites her lip as I walk closer, wishing that lip were in my mouth.

"What kind of payment do you have in mind? Because I do like things dirty," she says with a twinkle in her eye.

"Dirty, it is then," I say.

I slip out of my shorts, and I walk over to my dresser where I keep a stash of condoms. I grab one and then walk straight to Sloane before throwing her over my shoulder. Then, I head out to the outdoor shower. I don't put her down until we are both in the shower, and then I flick the water on, drenching us both with cold water that I know better than anyone is going to take at least ten minutes before it resembles anything close to lukewarm.

I'm used to it, but Sloane screams as the cold water rains down on us. I kiss her, knowing that is the best way to warm her up. We both forget about the cold water as my hands are finally able to grab her bare breasts. As we are finally together, completely naked, skin on skin. If the beach was perfection, being with her now in the water is magical.

"I need you inside me—now. I know I just had you, but now that I've had a taste of you, I want you more than I did before," she says.

I grin. "But I haven't had a taste of you yet."

I lift her up and press her back against the wall so that I can bury my head in her pussy. She grabs hold of my head, encouraging me to keep at it. To fuck her with my mouth, my tongue. To make her scream, to make her come. She comes quickly with the flick of my tongue and the cold water pounding down on top of her.

I lower her and then flip her around so that her back is to me before I enter her.

"Yes, Asher!"

I don't last long inside her. And, somehow, she manages to come again and again as I thrust inside her. When we have both come and there is nothing left but the water pouring down over us, I reach for the soap to attempt to get the sand properly off of us. I know, realistically, it is going to take days to get it off, and if she decides to spend her next few days mostly at the beach, like I do, she is never going to be able to fully get rid of the sand.

I take the bar of soap and start slowly moving it over her body, washing her. Getting to know every inch of her skin, the smell of her hair, the curves of her body. She doesn't say a word as I do so. She just lets me take care of her, and it seems more intimate than any other time we have had together.

When I have touched every part of her body with the bar of soap, she takes it from my hand and does the same to me. Our eyes are locked. When she finishes, she shivers.

"Does the water ever warm up?" she asks to give a reason for her shiver.

I know her shiver has more to do with our intimate moment than with the cold water.

"Not really," I say.

She nods and then swallows hard so that I can see her throat moving. I imagine my cock down her throat, and my dick instantly becomes hard.

When my eyes go back to hers, I see something different there. More serious than before.

"Marry me," she says.

My whole world stops. I can't breathe, and I'm afraid my heart has stopped.

"Marry me."

Two words that I never thought I would hear or ever say to any woman.

But this woman is different. Sloane is different, so I know, when she says those two words, there is more to this story than I understand. She didn't preface it by saying she loved me, which there is no way for her to have fallen in love with me so quickly. She's not like the other girls. That isn't what she wants. She has a reason for asking me that she just hasn't told me yet.

I surprise myself by even considering saying yes, but it could get me more sex and a chance to really destroy her later if I decide I want to.

She thinks I'm predictable. She hates surprises, or so she says, but that just makes me want to surprise her even more.

So, I say the one word that I know will shock her the most, "Yes."

TWELVE

Sloane

He said yes.

I don't think I can believe that word. He just said it to shock me. I know him well enough to know that. I know he doesn't want to get married—ever. I just asked him because I couldn't hold it in any longer. I needed to ask. I need him to know the truth.

"Yes? That's your answer? Just like that? You don't even want to have a discussion about it or ask why I am proposing marriage when, only hours ago, I was engaged and going to get married to another man the next day."

He grins.

Damn it, I hate his grin. It makes me do things I never thought I would. It makes me feel things I shouldn't. Asher is a dick, an asshole. I have to remember that above everything else. I have to stay strong and not let him influence me. This is just an arrangement to solve my problem, nothing more. That's what I have to convince him of anyway. Even if my heart flutters much too fast anytime I am around him.

"I'm sure I'll figure out why you want me to marry you soon enough. I know enough about you to know that there is a very clear reason why. And I know that reason has nothing to do with love. But at least it gives me another shot at fucking you in the shower, on the beach, and on every inch of this place and yours before we are through."

Damn it.

He grins again, and all I can think about is how much I want him to fuck me in his bed, my bed, and every other surface that we can come across. And I hate him for making me want him when I should still be in love with Wes.

He turns off the water that never really got warm and then hands me a towel from the rack that is just outside the shower. Our fingers brush against each other. And I can see in his eyes how much he wants to dry me off but doesn't want to overstep his bounds. He thinks he's pushed his luck already by washing me. And he's probably right. I need to dry myself off and gain some control over my life again. Especially if we are going to have any sort of serious conversation instead of jumping each other again for the third time in an hour.

I take the towel and quickly dry off before wrapping it around my body. Asher does the same, and then we head back inside his home. I'm still not sure I believe him when he says this is his only place. It can't be. He says he doesn't lie, but I don't imagine he stays here year-round. He uses this place when he is surfing and wants to be near the beach. Or when he's trying to get rid of his latest one-night stand. But this can't be where he spends most of his time. There simply isn't enough room.

I take a seat on what he calls a couch. Although I don't think it can be considered a couch. It's barely held together. There are no longer any legs on the bottom, the stuffing has settled so that there is a hole in the middle, and the fabric covering it is worn and contains mostly holes.

Asher goes over to his dresser and pulls out a pair of boxer shorts and a T-shirt. He tosses them both to me and then pulls out another pair of boxer shorts. He drops his towel like I'm not even here and begins to put the boxer shorts on.

I look down at the clothes he just tossed to me. They would be much more comfortable to wear than my dress I came here in, and I can't stay in this towel forever. But it just seems too intimate to be wearing his clothing.

"What? Don't tell me you're getting shy on me now," Asher says, raising an eyebrow.

I stand and drop my towel to the ground, showing my naked body to him. I'm not the least bit concerned with what he thinks of me or my body. And then I put the clothes on that he tossed to me. I try not to smell his scent on them. I try not to seem affected.

Asher comes over and takes a seat next to me, not seeming the least bit concerned about why I asked him to marry him. Or what our future holds. He slings his arm over the back of the couch.

I smile. I can't help it when his hand grazes the back of my neck.

"So, let's hear it. I know you are dying to tell me and to get everything straightened out. I can see it in your eyes. You want to talk about us getting married," he says.

I take a deep breath. "I do."

We chuckle, both a bit nervous.

"Well?" he asks.

"I have to get married," I say.

He chuckles. "I doubt that. You seem more than independent enough, and I know you don't need a man to keep you company. And you are more than capable of making enough money on your own; therefore, you don't need a man to take care of you either. And I know calling off the wedding must be embarrassing, but your family and friends will get over it soon enough. So, why in the world would you have to get married?"

I frown. "Fine. I don't have to get married. But I have a proposition for you. Marry me for one year. It will help me ease the embarrassment of turning down Wes. I could say we used to date years ago and rekindled our love when I found out Wes was really an ass. The company and I could really use some good press. We've been struggling to get new donors, and as sexist as it is, the company will get more donations if I have a man by my side. The press thinks I'm going to die alone. They are already comparing me to my grandmother, who spent most of her life living with just her cats."

Asher laughs. "You're serious."

I nod.

"You want me to marry you to save face?"

"Yes."

"And what do I get out of all of this?"

I think for a moment. "A chance to become a better person instead of a thief who tries to steal women who are already taken."

He frowns, and I can see that it's not enough.

"And you can teach me how to live again. How to enjoy life and be a bit of a wild child again instead of the uptight snob I currently am."

Asher chuckles again. "You, a wild child? I don't believe it's possible for you to have been anything but the perfect child growing up."

I shake my head. "Well then, you'd be wrong. I was a complete wild child, always getting into trouble. Trust me."

"I doubt you were a true wild child. I imagine your parents thought that because you wouldn't eat your vegetables or something silly like that."

"No, it was much worse than that. Anyway, my grandmother was the one who convinced me that I shouldn't continue my wild ways into adulthood. She gave me a job at the company, and I finally realized my purpose. I worked my way up the company, almost the same as anyone else. Although I know I was given an easier time than most since I was related to my grandmother."

"Why would I want to help you? I still don't see anything in this for me."

"Money then. I'll pay you. You could actually live in a nice place on the beach."

He grins. "Sweetheart, you forget that I make plenty of money. And I prefer living this way."

"That's not what I've heard. I've heard that your sponsors are starting to drop out because of a certain reputation you have with the ladies. They think it's inappropriate to work with someone like you. So, being married might help your reputation and help you make more money."

He shakes his head. "Again, like I said, I don't need any more money."

But I can see that he is at least thinking about what I said. I've struck a nerve, but it's still not enough.

I look around the room he calls home. I doubt he's telling me the full story about this. But I can see I'm getting nowhere.

His eyes drop to my chest to see my nipples harden as a cold draft slips through. Now, it's my turn to grin because I know the way to get what I want.

"Sex. You can have all the dirty, filthy sex with me you want."

His eyes perk up as he listens. And I can see the bulge in his boxers grow.

"Did you ever love Wes?"

His question surprises me.

"*Love* is a strange word. I loved him, sure. But was I in love with him? No, I don't think so. I would have ended it much sooner if I wasn't so much of a planner that I wanted to be married by twenty-five and have two kids by the time I was thirty."

He frowns.

"I don't want to have kids with you. I just don't want to feel like a complete failure when I do turn twenty-five next month. I want to be married and have that experience. If, after you, I still don't find my happily ever after with a man, then I'll be fine with adopting or getting artificial insemination."

Asher frowns, thinking.

"I know that we are the absolute worst match for each other and that this is going to be mostly about sex, but I need that right now. I need to be married. I need to not be shamed by my family. I need sex."

I fidget with the hem of the shirt I'm wearing, where it is already starting to unravel. It's obviously a shirt that he wears often.

"So, what do you say? Can we come to an agreement? Will you marry me?" I don't add that it's the least he can do after he broke up my wedding, but I'm not afraid to sound desperate.

Asher chuckles. "I already said yes. But I will say it again if the first time didn't do enough to convince you. Yes, I'll marry you. I'll give you whatever you want. Just..." He pauses, trying to think of the right words.

"Just don't expect you to stick around forever?"

He nods.

"Fine. I'll have my lawyer draw up a prenup to protect us both, and then we can get married anytime after that. I don't want a big affair. I just want the legal marriage so that I can face the world again. But you will have to stay loyal to me. I don't do cheating even if this is a temporary arrangement. It won't last forever anyway. I expect, after a year, we can quietly divorce, and I can marry someone else and have a kid or two."

"I would never cheat on you."

I raise an eyebrow. "That's not what I've heard. I've heard you have cheated on plenty of women."

He scoots closer to me on the couch. "I. Don't. Cheat. On. Anyone. And. Especially. Not. You. Occasionally, women I have been with cheat on their husbands or fiancés with me, but I never do the cheating."

"I didn't cheat on Wes, if that is what you are implying. I broke up with him first."

He smiles. "I'm not calling you a cheater either."

"Have you ever been in a committed relationship with a woman before?" I ask.

He laughs. "Of course I have. What do you think I've been doing these last few weeks? I've been committed to you."

"To breaking me and Wes up."

He nods and leans back a little, like he's preparing for me to slap him. And, although I've had the urge to do just that many times in the past, I don't have the urge at the moment.

Maybe it's because he just gave me two of the best orgasms of my life. Maybe it's because, when this conversation is over, I want to see if he has anything else up his sleeve.

Whatever the reason, I no longer feel like slapping him, but I don't want to let him know that. I like that he feels like he should always be on alert when he's around me. I like having that control.

"Do you have anything planned for tomorrow?" I ask.

"Other than having you tied up in my bed all day, I don't have anything on the agenda."

I smile. "Good. You can do that—after we get married."

He grins and then leans forward and kisses me, letting me know he's ready for another round if I am.

But all I can think is, *I can't believe my crazy plan is working. Now, the only thing I need to do to keep this plan working is to not fall in love with him. That should be easy, right?*

THIRTEEN

Sloane

I look in the mirror at myself in my wedding dress. I'm not the type of woman who dreamed of what my wedding day would look like. What I would wear or even whom I would marry. But, if I had imagined what I would wear, this is what I would have imagined.

A simple, light white dress with a little bit of lace but not enough to overpower the dress. It's long but doesn't have a train, so it will be easy to wear on the beach. I'm not wearing shoes, which is how I prefer it so that I can walk barefoot on the beach. And, other than a couple of witnesses the minister is bringing, no one will be there to watch us get married.

The man, on the other hand, is nothing like I would have imagined ever marrying. I figured the only way I would ever marry was if the man had really convinced me of his love and if I thought that love would last. I never thought I would get married out of lust or a need to fix things.

I hear a rattling on my door, and I walk over to it and open it to find my lawyer standing there.

"You look beautiful," Chance says, looking me up and down in my dress.

"Thank you. Were you able to get the prenup written up?"

"Of course. I wouldn't be here if I hadn't finished it. It's just as we discussed. But I know you will want a chance to read it over all the same."

"Thank you. I trust you, but I could never sign something I didn't read over with my own eyes."

"That's why I enjoy working with you so much. You take your business and life into your own hands."

Chance hands me the papers, and I take them over to my table and begin reading through everything. It takes me a good half hour to thoroughly read over everything. Chance waits in the living room while I read in my office. I make one small change, but otherwise, everything looks to be exactly as I wanted.

I hear another knock at my door, and I glance at the clock in my bedroom. It's a good thing I was ready prior to my lawyer coming over.

I glance in the mirror one last time. I left my hair down in loose curls and kept my makeup natural-looking. Everything is still in place, so I walk quickly to the door and open it to see Asher standing in the doorway.

His jaw drops open, and his eyes widen when he sees me in my dress. "There are not enough words to describe how beautiful you look right now."

"You look very nice as well," I say, staring at the muscles of his chest.

There's just enough manly hair peeking out from beneath his nicely pressed dress shirt that he's kept unbuttoned at the top. He rolled up the sleeves and is wearing khaki pants and sandals.

He raises an eyebrow, as he always does when he is about to

say something snarky. "Nice? I look better than nice. I look hot, and you know you want to jump my bones before you even marry me."

I shake my head. "Business first."

He pouts. "Not even—"

I swat his hand away that reached out to try and grab my ass. "First, we sign the prenup and then get married. If I still like you, you can fuck me."

"I'd better hurry and make sure all the legal parts are covered then. I don't want to get in the way of the fucking," Chance says, smiling.

I frown even though I've been friends with Chance forever, and he works for me on many occasions. I still don't like him joking about me and Asher fucking.

Chance and Asher exchange knowing glances before I head to my office to grab the prenup papers. When I come back, I get straight down to business, not wanting to wait any longer to get this part over with.

I place the papers on my dining table, and Chance takes them.

"It's a standard prenup that basically says that when—"

I glare at Chance. I haven't told anyone of my plan, and even though I know that our marriage is going to end in divorce, I don't like others implying it already. Even Chance.

"I mean, *if* you two decide to dissolve the marriage, it basically states that you will each keep your own property and money that you earned before the marriage and during. Sloane has already read it over, but if you'd like to have a quick read through it," Chance says, sliding the papers over to where Asher is standing.

"Do you have a pen?" Asher asks.

Chance smiles as he looks at me, like he knows I'm marrying an idiot who doesn't even read a contract before he signs it. But then Asher comes from a different world. Other than whatever contract he signed with his agent, I doubt he has ever signed anything of importance.

Chance hands Asher a pen, and then he points to the first spot that Asher needs to sign. "You need to sign here and then initial every page. Then, sign again at the end."

Asher does so without reading a single word on any page and then hands the pen to me. "There is no backing out after this. I guess we will just have to learn to trust each other."

I take the pen and quickly sign everywhere that I'm supposed to.

Chance takes the papers and scans them, making sure everything is in order. "So, when's the wedding?" he asks.

I cock my head to the side as I look at Chance.

"I'm kidding. Go get married, you two crazy lovebirds. I know that I'm not invited, but I'm sure I'll see you again soon," Chance says as he begins heading toward the door.

"That's because no one is invited. It's more romantic that way," I say.

"I'm sure it is," Chance answers before letting himself out of my apartment.

"Was that a stab at me, saying that our marriage won't last?" Asher asks.

"Yes. I didn't tell him the truth. He just has his suspicions. Why, do you think this marriage is going to last?" I ask.

Asher hesitantly touches my arm, running his fingers slowly up my arm, like he's trying to decide if I'm real. If what we are about to do is really happening. And then he firmly grabs my arm, pulling me to him until our lips clash together and then kiss. My tongue slips into his mouth almost automatically, like I've been kissing him for years instead of only hours.

He smells of cologne, which I find strange but also so enticing on him. When I had him yesterday, he smelled of salt and ocean. Now, he smells like a man who spends his days in an office instead of out on the beach. I don't know which I like more —this cleaned up version or the dressed down version on the beach. No, I prefer the naked version who likes to take control in bed.

The part that made me want to marry him in the first place was knowing that I would get to fuck him every night while we were together. That's what makes this all worthwhile for me.

We stop kissing.

"It won't last, but I am going to more than enjoy it while it does."

I blush. "Come on. The minister is waiting." I start walking toward the door. "Unless you want to back out?" I ask, turning back to see Asher still standing, looking at me with his hands in his pockets.

"Not backing out. Just admiring your ass in that dress and all the different ways I plan on bending you over and taking you."

In complete silence, we walk down to the beach where we are to be married. I'm still not sure he is going to actually go through with this. He's known to be one to try and break women's hearts. And I suspect he thinks, if he marries me and then breaks up with me later, it will make my pain that much worse. But he can't hurt me if I don't let him. He can't break my heart if I don't let myself love him.

As we walk though, I have a strange feeling that this is the worst idea I've had in a long time. I've never felt that marriage is important. My parents got divorced when I was young. Most of my friends' parents are divorced. I'm not sure we are really supposed to be with one person all our lives. But, walking down to the beach with Asher, who will be my husband in a matter of minutes, makes me doubt everything I've thought before.

Asher grabs hold of my hand as we get closer to the minister, who is standing at the edge of the water with folded arms over a Bible. I suck in a breath when he grabs hold of my hand. I don't know why his touch affects me, calms me, but it does.

Asher is the devil. I know that. But, somehow, the devil is what I need in a moment like this. Knowing who my enemy is and not being surprised by it, I guess, comforts me.

We reach the minister, but neither of us lets go of each other's hand.

"Are you both ready?" he asks us.

Asher turns to face me with a large grin on his face that makes me grin as well.

"Yes," we say in unison.

The minister starts talking, but the butterflies in my stomach prevent me from hearing anything he says.

Asher leans down to my ear and whispers, "Just look at the ocean. The waves. It will help calm you."

I smile. I don't think anything can calm me. But I look out at the ocean and watch the waves roll in, and then I immediately feel calm. It feels nice to know that, that is one thing we share. We both love the ocean.

And to fuck, the dirty side of me thinks.

"Do you, Sloane Hart, take Asher Calder to be your husband in sickness and health as long as you both shall live?"

I look into Asher's eyes and see the waves reflected in them. "I do," I say.

His eyes seem to twinkle just a little bit. Like he's happy to hear it. I push the butterflies down. The look doesn't mean anything. He is just doing this for the sex and to try and hurt me. That's all this is.

"I do," Asher says with a grin so wide that I'm afraid his mouth is going to be stuck permanently like that.

I feel my heartbeat race much too fast in my chest as Asher kisses me, holding me in his arms as he dips me backward, sucking all of my breath away. He slowly lets me back up.

"We're married," I whisper.

"We are, Mrs. Calder. Or are you not planning on taking my name?" he says with a wink.

I bite my lip and blush a little. "I think I'll be keeping my name."

Asher lifts me up, and I let out a high-pitched gasp.

It's a wonder I can breathe at all after the ceremony. Thank God it was fast, or I'm sure that I would have passed out from the mix of the sun bearing down on me and my inability to breathe.

It's too late to back out now though. I'm married. I just hope I made my life easier instead of harder.

Asher twirls me around, and for the first time since I was a kid, I feel like a princess. It's not a feeling I ever thought I would want to experience. Not at my age. But I love the freeing feeling it gives me until I realize what Asher is doing.

"No!" I scream, grabbing hold of his neck and shoulders.

But it's no use. He drops us both into the water. We go under, all the way until the water is covering our heads. When we come back up, I know my dress and makeup are ruined, but I can't help but laugh when I see Asher's goofy face.

"That was way too serious. I thought we needed to chill out and laugh before we left," Asher says, still holding me in his arms.

I throw my arms and head back, floating on top of the water. "We don't need to leave yet. You'll have plenty of time to fuck me later. Now that you have gotten me into the water, I don't want to leave," I say, relaxing on top of the water.

"Well, I hate to tell you, but you don't have much time to

relax. But you'll have plenty of time to relax and fuck later," he says.

I stand up and look at him. "I have no idea what you are talking about, Asher. The only thing on either of our agendas today was to get married. Now that, that is done, we can relax." I pause. "Actually, the last thing we need to do is tell our families that we eloped."

"Already done," Asher says.

I frown. "How is it already done? I haven't spoken to my family today. Did you already talk to your family?"

"I don't have any family. I only have one friend. I texted him, but I don't think he believed me. I let my agent know so that she would be prepared to deal with the publicity."

I sigh. "I still need to tell my family."

"No, you don't."

I laugh. "I think they deserve to know if I got married or not."

Asher shakes his head. "I just meant that I already told them."

"What do you mean?" I ask, my eyes wide with worry.

"I called and spoke to your father to ask for his permission to marry you. Well, more his blessing than permission. I think asking for permission is a bit archaic."

"And?" I ask, cocking my head to one side, not believing that he spoke to my father.

"And he seemed pleased that you had found someone to marry. Even a scoundrel like me."

I smile.

"I spoke to your mother as well. She seemed more than pleased that she could tell all of your family that you got married to a longtime friend you had known since you were young. A love that rekindled after Wes treated you so badly. She also said it would be announced in the papers tomorrow to combat any bad press about you leaving Wes the night before you were supposed to marry him."

I study Asher, who seems so at peace in the ocean. He seems so right here, in the water, and it's why he sometimes seems so out of place on land. I know that he's a scoundrel, just like my father called him, but honestly, I've seen too much of his nicer side to think of him solely as a scoundrel.

"Thank you," I say.

He softly kisses me on the lips, clearly not wanting to start something here. And, looking around at the beach that is beginning to swarm with people, I agree.

"You really need to stop saying thank you."

"Then, you need to stop being so nice to me."

Asher glances up at something on the beach. I turn to look but have no idea what he is looking at.

"We need to head back in now," Asher says.

"Why?"

"I'm not telling you. But, now that you are my wife, you have to do what you are told. It's in the vows or something, right?"

I laugh. "No way in hell am I obeying you. And it wasn't in the vows." *Was it?*

He laughs. "You have no idea what that minister guy said anyway, do you?"

"No, I don't."

"So, are you going to come with me without asking questions or not?"

I frown, not liking where this is going at all.

"I thought you wanted me to bring out that wild child inside of you again, the one looking for excitement and adventure?"

I frown. "I don't like surprises."

"I know." He lifts me in his arms again and begins carrying me out of the water. I fight to get down at first, but I know it's no use. So, I surrender to Asher carrying me up to the beach like a caveman.

When he reaches dry land, I say, "You can put me down now."

"Not going to happen."

I sigh and try to enjoy being in his strong arms. I try to relax and just give up control. But I struggle to let go of the control even though I know he isn't really in control. I was the one who orchestrated this. I'm the one in control. I suck in a breath, but he is the one that smells so amazing.

He carries me back up to my condo before he puts me down. "You have five minutes to get changed into something dry and comfortable."

I frown. "I need longer than five minutes. I'm a mess. My makeup is smeared, and my hair is a mess from the salt water. And, if you tell me what we are doing, then I can be better dressed for the occasion."

He shakes his head. "Five minutes. Wipe the makeup off your face. Your hair is perfect the way it is. And wear something comfortable, like jeans and a T-shirt."

I don't know why I agree to what he said, but I do. I strip out of my wet wedding dress, leaving it crumpled on the floor. I long for a warm shower to wash off the salt water, but I know I don't have time. If I shower, I'll be in there for much longer than five minutes, and as much as I don't want to admit it, I want to find out what Asher has planned. And, if I'm not ready in five minutes, then I'm not sure I'll get to find out the surprise.

So, instead, I throw on a pair of jeans and a light blouse instead of a T-shirt because, honestly, I feel more comfortable a bit dressed up. I feel strange even wearing jeans. I only own two pair anyway. And then I head to the bathroom to try my best to get rid of the makeup and fix my hair.

I scrub at my face with makeup remover until it is clean

again. And then I run a brush through my wet hair before scrunching it to give it a little bit of a natural curl as it dries. I pinch my cheeks to ensure some color and apply a little lip gloss. But that is all I have time for as much as I want to do more.

I head out of my bedroom and find Asher standing in my living room. He's now in khaki shorts, a T-shirt, and flip-flops, looking much more like himself.

He shakes his head. "You had to defy me just a little bit, didn't you?"

"I did exactly what you said. I got ready in five minutes, despite wanting to take a nice long bath to rinse off."

"I said, a T-shirt."

I smile. "Well, you need to get used to me not listening to everything you say. Now that we are married and all."

He walks toward me, his eyes challenging me. I stand my ground until he is inches from my face.

"I wish I had time to punish you."

I grin. "That isn't going to get me to obey you in the future."

He slightly shakes his head. "I know. But I would enjoy punishing you all the same." He grabs my hand. "Come on, or we will miss our flight."

I step back. "What do you mean, flight? I don't have any luggage. I haven't let the company know that I'll be gone. How long will we be gone? Where are we going? You can't just spring shit like this on me..."

Asher just stands stoically with a large grin on his face and an eyebrow raised as he waits for me to stop talking. When I let my questions trail off, he says, "Are you finished?"

"Yes," I say, nodding.

"We are going on a honeymoon, as is expected. I have handled everything. This is me holding up my end of the deal to help you find the part of you that likes adventure and needs to let go more."

I frown. I didn't expect him to move so quickly on holding up his end of the bargain. I know that this is what I need.

"So, are you coming with me or not?"

"I'm coming," I answer as confidently as I can muster.

I don't trust at all that he has gotten everything figured out. But I can call from the plane and have someone at work handle all the business things that need handling this week or for however long we are staying. This week, I just need to enjoy myself.

I step into the elevator, still holding on to Asher's hand. He presses the button for the ground floor, and the doors close, locking us inside. I feel trapped, like there is no escaping now. I need to stop worrying about it now though. Now, I just have to enjoy the ride and try not to fall in love with the handsome stranger whose hand I'm holding.

FOURTEEN

Sloane

"Venice. Is that really where we are going, or is it one stop on many?" I ask as I take my seat next to Asher on the flight to Venice.

He sighs. "I can see that you are going to drive me crazy with questions from now until the trip ends."

"Yep," I reply.

Asher rolls his eyes. "Fine. We are starting in Venice because I heard it's beautiful and romantic, and I figured that is what is needed for our first night as a married couple."

My heart is racing in my chest as I think about what Venice is going to be like. I live in one of the most beautiful places on the planet and have traveled extensively on business, usually to the poorest places in the world. But, now, I get to go experience the beauty of another place.

"And then?" I ask because it seems like there is more up his sleeve than just going to Venice.

"And then we are going to backpack across Europe. Stay wherever we can find a place to stay or sleep in a tent. It will be a great adventure, waking up every night in a new place, not knowing where or what we are going to be doing the next day."

I smile, but it doesn't sound at all exciting. It sounds terrifying. I like control too much to be okay with his plan. Maybe once we get to Venice, we will love it so much that we just stay there. Or maybe I can arrange for us to visit several places in Europe while we are there.

Asher grabs my hand and kisses me on the lips. My eyes close when his lips touch mine, and I feel the softness of his lips before his tongue moves with mine.

When he leans back, he grins. "Are you relaxed now?"

"Mmhmm," I say with a goofy smile on my face.

He quickly kisses me on the forehead. "Stop worrying. Stop trying to control everything. Just relax."

I lean my head back in my chair and close my eyes, trying to do just that. When I open them again, I see Asher staring at me. Happy to be doing nothing more than just watching me, it seems.

He slowly puts his arm around me, and I settle in against his chest and close my eyes.

"Just sleep. When you wake up, we will be in a whole new world."

I smile and take a deep breath as I close my eyes. Immediately, I feel sleep coming for me. I didn't realize how tiring it was to plan two weddings this week. But, for now, I get to sleep.

It's early morning by the time we land in Venice. I slept almost the whole flight, only waking when they served us breakfast before we landed. I have no idea how Asher managed the flight. I slept against his hard chest, and somehow, he must have slept, too, because he seems to be just as rested as I am when we depart the plane.

As we leave the cab that brought us to our hotel in the heart of the city, I don't get to focus on how beautiful the city is. Instead, all I can think and worry about is how there is no way he brought everything that I'd need in the single backpack that he has slung over his back. No way.

Asher rolls his eyes at me and takes my hand, like I'm a five-year-old child he has to corral. He leads me into the lobby of the hotel and over to the front desk.

"Are you checking in?" the man behind the desk asks in English with a sharp Italian accent.

He can already tell that we are American tourists, just from looking at us.

"Yes. I'm Asher Calder."

"Ah, the honeymooners!" the man says.

He grabs a key that looks to be an actual key, not a card, and that's when I realize this isn't a hotel. At least not what I think of when I think of hotels.

The man starts scurrying us along as he starts speaking in Italian, much too fast for either of us to understand. But we follow until we get to a room at the top of the stairs. The man opens the door for us with a large smile on his face. He hands Asher the key and then says something else I can't make out before leaving us here.

Asher sets the backpack down on a chair as we both look around the room. It's beautiful. Smaller than I'm used to but definitely full of beauty and charm. It feels as if we stepped into a different time though. The bed looks to be an antique although the bedspread is a beautiful material of red and gold. The nightstands also look to be solid wood with deep carvings on them, nothing like the stark coldness of hotel rooms back home.

I see a door to what I assume is the bathroom, but I don't look inside. Instead, I follow Asher out onto the balcony that is attached to our room, and my jaw drops. The balcony is small. Just big enough for both of us to be out here with a tiny table and set of chairs, perfect for two people to sit on.

But, my God, the view.

"It's like nothing I've ever seen before," I say as I place my hand on the edge of the balcony and look down at the river below.

Asher's fingers brush against mine, and then I feel his eyes on me. "Like nothing I have ever seen before either."

I suck in a breath, but I love hearing his words all the same even if they are a lie. I want to feel loved even if I can't fall in love back. And lines like that show that Asher is one step closer to falling in love with me.

I grab Asher's neck at the same time as he grabs my hips, and we press our lips together in a passionate kiss, agreeing that we need this more than exploring Venice. We need it as much or more than the air we breathe. We need sex. We need that connection that we haven't had since yesterday evening before we were married.

His tongue slips into my mouth, and he has me moaning and wet with just his tongue in my mouth and not yet on other places. I cry silently to myself, thanking God that I get to have this man completely to myself. I don't think about the fact that this is a temporary arrangement. That he isn't really mine forever. He's mine for now, and that's enough.

Although I could kiss him for hours, I need more. Now. I need his tongue all over my body. I need to see his muscles flexing as he moves inside me. I need to feel his hard dick pressing into my soul. I've been with plenty of men before, but for some reason, I think Asher could show me things that none of the others ever have before. He's made me come more in one day than Wes did in a year. Although I'd never admit it to Asher. His ego is already too large.

I grab hold of his shirt and begin pulling it up, loving how my fingers ripple over the ridges of his abs as I move the shirt higher and higher. Wes was in shape. But nothing like Asher is. I pull the shirt off and stop kissing him long enough to properly admire him. Now that we are married, I can gawk at him without feeling ashamed.

I suck in a breath as my eyes soak in every bit of his body.

"Strip naked, so I can get a better look at you, and then fuck me," I say.

He chuckles. "You dirty girl."

He doesn't do what I asked though. Instead, he lifts me, carrying me in his arms back inside. "I'll fuck you anyplace, anywhere. But I'm not going to fuck you on a hard balcony where anyone could glimpse your body. Not when we have a nice soft bed just inside."

I'm surprised at how gently he is carrying me. It's almost romantic. Not that I think this man has a romantic bone in his body. But, still, it's a nice feeling.

Asher gently tosses me on the bed. "Strip."

I smile. I hate admitting that, as much as I want to be in control in almost everything in my life, I love having Asher boss me around.

"No," I say because I want to hear him order me around again.

His eyes darken just a little as he glares at me. "Strip, or I won't make you come."

I frown. "You play dirty."

"I thought you liked it dirty," he says, winking.

I suck in a breath and then take off my shirt.

He grins when I finally give in. I quickly take off my bra and start moving to my jeans when Asher starts stripping as well.

And, suddenly, I move much slower with my own clothes because my eyes are too transfixed on him instead of the task at hand.

"Strip," Asher says again more firmly.

I move quicker until I'm completely naked and lying on the bed. Asher grabs a bottle of champagne that I didn't see chilling when we first came into the room. He moves to the backpack on the floor and pulls out a condom. He picks up his T-shirt for some reason before he walks toward me.

As he walks, my eyes drink in every bit of his hard body. His cock is already hard, waiting for me. He sets the condom and bottle down on the end table next to the bed. He takes his T-shirt in his hand as he straddles me, his cock pressing into my stomach.

He takes the T-shirt and moves it over my eyes.

I frown. "I want to see you."

"You will. Just not with your eyes."

He ties the T-shirt over my eyes, and other than another pout, I don't protest. I let him cover my eyes. I let him be in control.

I feel his lips on mine, rewarding me for letting him put the blindfold on. His lips move to my neck, and the feeling is more intense than anything I have ever felt before.

I bite my lip to keep from moaning too loudly. I'm not sure how insulated the walls are, but I don't want our neighbors to hear me.

Suddenly, I feel cold liquid trailing over my breasts, followed by his lips warming the liquid as it moves over my breasts. The difference between the hot and cold sends shivers down my spine.

"I want to properly enjoy every bit of your body, Sloane. I didn't get the chance to earlier."

I take a deep breath in and out. "I don't know if I can wait until you have properly enjoyed every bit of my body."

I feel his grin against the peak of one of my nipples as I squirm beneath his touch. I grab hold of the nape of his neck, trying to push his head down to fully take my nipple in his mouth instead of teasing me like he is. He does relent though, and I squirm as his tongue expertly glides over my nipple that is covered in the cool liquid.

"Fuck, Asher," I say, my toes curling, as he moves to the other hard peak.

I feel more of the cold liquid over my smooth stomach, going down my body with his warm lips moving it around, igniting every nerve in my body. The liquid moves down one leg, and his lips trace the liquid down, making me come unglued at his touch.

"Don't move," he says.

His lips start moving down my inner thigh, and I can't help but squirm.

"I. Can't. Help. It. I need—"

But Asher already knows where I'm going with my moans. His tongue and lips encase my pussy as I moan and pray for him to never stop what he is doing. Never. Because I've never had a man move his tongue over my clit like this man is doing now.

I thought sex with him was good before, but now that I've had his lips on my pussy, I can't imagine that my days of feeling like this are numbered. That I won't get to experience this every day for forever.

I shake the thought away though as his tongue moves faster over my clit just as he slips a finger inside me.

"My God, Asher," I say, barely able to get the words out.

"Don't come. Not yet, sweetheart."

My whole body tenses, trying to do as he asked. To not come

until he tells me to come. But, every second, I inch closer to coming and not caring about disobeying him.

He must sense how close I am because he stops. And, suddenly, his body isn't touching me anywhere. I take a deep breath in and out, in and out, trying to slow my beating heart, as I wait for Asher to touch me.

He doesn't. He takes his damn time because he has more patience than anyone on the planet. He must have patience to have me naked, lying in front of him, and not fucking me immediately. I know he wants to fuck me just as badly as I want to fuck him.

I reach up, trying to touch him.

"Stop," he says as soon as I move.

I do.

"Patience," he says. "Trust me," he whispers in my ear.

I nod a little, letting him know that I do, despite everything I know about him. Knowing how horrible of a person he really is, I do trust him. At least I do with my body. He has more than proven he is capable of handling that.

So, I try to be patient. I try to think about what adventures we are going to have in Venice. But, for the life of me, I can't remember what Venice is famous for or even what country I am in at the moment.

All I can think about is Asher. His grin. His abs. His cock. And how much I want—no, *need* him to fuck me right now. Every nerve in my body is alive and on fire. Every part of me aches to be his. Every part of me is begging for him to do more. Touch me. Kiss me. Fuck me.

Anything. Just do anything.

I hear him move. Barely, but I hear it. I hear him opening the condom wrapper, and I assume—no, *hope* that he is rolling it onto his cock.

He moves. He's in control. He didn't tie me up. I can move if I want to, but somehow, he controls me all the same. I don't move because he told me not to.

I feel him climb back on top of me. I feel his cock settle in between my legs. I feel his breath on my neck. And I know, if he so much as whispered the word *come*, I would in a second without him even touching me.

"Take me," he says as he finally pushes inside me. His lips kiss my neck as he fills me.

I try to stifle my cries and moans.

"Scream, Sloane. Tell me how much you want this."

I let out a cry of pure ecstasy that I'm sure is much too loud, but I don't care because Asher told me to.

"Not yet," he says as he thrusts inside me.

I stop screaming and go back to biting my lip and curling my toes to keep from coming. I've never been blindfolded before, but now that I am, I'm not sure I want to go back to seeing. Because losing my sight has made everything that much better. I can see with my whole body.

He moves again, and I suck in a breath, but I know I can't keep from coming any longer.

"Come, Sloane."

I do as he screams, "Fuck, baby!"

We both come, and then he collapses on top of me. He removes the blindfold as we catch our breaths, and we stare into each other's eyes.

"I don't think I'm ever going to get enough of fucking you, Sloane."

I grin and bite my lip because I don't think I'm ever going to get enough of him either. And, as much as we are compatible when it comes to sex, we aren't one in any other way. I can't fall in love, or even lust, with him because this isn't going to last.

~

We can't keep our hands off of each other as we walk down the street to the closest café. One fuck isn't enough to satisfy either of us.

"If your stomach hadn't growled three times while I was fucking you, I would still have you in my bed right now, finding every possible way to keep fucking you," Asher whispers into my ear.

I grin. "Then, we must eat quickly."

Asher shakes his head as he drinks in my body again. I'm wearing a simple sundress that Asher packed for me. He brought one dress, one pair of jeans, one pair of shorts, a few pairs of underwear, and my toothbrush. Everything else, he said we could buy or make do without. And it seems that we are going to be spending most of our time naked anyway. So, I guess it doesn't matter.

We are seated at a small table and have to break apart in order to sit down. But, as soon as the waitress leaves, Asher scoots his chair over so that he is sitting right next to me. He puts his arm around my shoulders as we both stare down at the menu that is in Italian.

"Do you have any idea what any of these things are or how to pronounce them?" I ask.

He shrugs. "Does it matter? We are in Italy. I'm sure whatever we order is going to be amazing."

"I don't think I care as long as I can fill my stomach and then get back to our hotel room," I say, winking.

He laughs. "I am not letting us go back to our hotel room until we have at least had a chance to explore more of Venice first."

I frown. "Then, you are going to have to fuck me in an alleyway because I'm not waiting past lunch to have you again."

Asher's eyes dart playfully from mine up to where our waiter is standing, looking at us with a bit of a shocked expression on his face. We might not understand Italian, but it is clear that he understands English.

"What can I get for you two lovebirds?" he asks, finally smiling at us after the initial shock of hearing me swear in front of him.

"Um..." I look down at the menu, not having a clue. I'm not the most adventurous person with my food.

Asher notices my expression. "We will each have a glass of wine. Whatever red you recommend for me and..." Asher looks at me, waiting for me to answer.

"White," I say.

"White for her. And we will have whatever you recommend for our meals. Something with a bit of variety would be good. We would love to try as much as we can."

"Excellent, sir. I'll have the chef prepare a sampler platter for you."

"Thank you," Asher and I say at the same time.

The waiter leaves and returns in seconds with a bottle of red and white wine that he pours for each of us. He leaves us again, and I open my mouth to say something when a basket of bread suddenly appears at our table.

Asher smiles at me and moves to hold my hand, but then he grabs for the bread instead. I laugh at his antics and then grab a piece of bread for myself.

"Oh God. This is the best damn thing I think I've ever tasted. Sorry, sweetheart, but this bread tastes better than you," Asher says.

I laugh again and take a bite of the bread, and I immediately fall in love. "I think I've just fallen in love with a piece of bread," I say with a mouthful of bread.

Asher laughs but shovels in more bread. I do the same.

The waiter comes back a few minutes later with two giant

plates of all sorts of different foods. My eyes grow wide as I look at all the food we're expected to eat.

"Bon appétit!" the waiter says before leaving us to eat our enormous meal.

We dig into the food. Neither of us speaks. We just eat. And eat and eat.

But, eventually, my stomach starts to grow full, and my hunger turns back to other needs. Asher is still shoveling in food, but I know he can't keep eating for much longer. He must be close to as full as I am at this point.

And I don't want him thinking that we are ready to go exploring just yet. I need to explore more of him before I spend any time exploring the town. I need a lot more of him. Like at least the rest of today, tonight, and part of tomorrow before I'm satiated enough to be able to focus on exploring the rest of the town. I just need to figure out how to get him on board with my plan.

We are seated outside on the patio of the restaurant. There are a couple of other couples here, but none seem to be paying us any attention. I know Paris is considered the place to go for love, but it looks to me like Venice might give Paris a run for its money.

I don't think anyone is going to be able to see me or even care if they do realize what I am doing. So, I take a chance. I slide as close as I can to Asher and slide my hand under the napkin in his lap. He doesn't look up from his plate. He just keeps shoveling in food until I slip my hand into the waistband of his pants. I find his cock, and within seconds, it starts to grow hard within my grasp as I massage him.

He cocks his head to one side and looks at me with a grin on his face. "Is that the way you are going to try and gain control back?"

I smile. "Is it working?"

He sucks in a sharp breath when I tighten my grip on his throbbing cock again.

"It depends on what you think a win is for you."

"Getting you to spend the rest of the day fucking me in our hotel room is a win. So, have I won yet? Or do I need to work *harder*?" I say, winking.

Asher adjusts his chair, forcing me to let him go. I frown as I watch him reach into his pocket and pull out some money. He waves our waiter down and hands him money, asking if it's enough. When the waiter nods, Asher grabs my hand, pulling me from my chair.

I grin as he does. I won. I knew I would. No man can resist, not once they are turned on, no matter how much they want to win.

We exit the restaurant and start walking the couple of blocks back to our hotel room when Asher pulls me abruptly into an alleyway. He pushes me up against the brick wall and kisses me harder than he ever has before. I can't breathe while he kisses me. It's too much and not enough all at the same time.

"What are you doing?" I ask when I can breathe again.

"I'm winning by fucking you here instead of in the hotel room."

I grin. "I don't care as long as you fuck me."

FIFTEEN

Sloane

Our plane lands back in Hawaii, and our fake honeymoon ends. Although we are back in paradise, we are back in the real world. Back to work where we can't just have sex every day and pretend like the real world doesn't exist. We have to get back to work, and I have to continue on with...

I don't even want to think about it.

All I want to think about is all the sex. Sex in our hotel room. Sex in the alleyway. Sex in the restroom of every restaurant we ate at. Sex on the balcony. We had more sex than I think I've ever had in a week's time.

And, even though we were in Italy and Asher planned on having us travel across Europe, I guess that is going to have to wait for another time, I think, smiling.

Because I wouldn't change our honeymoon for anything. I wouldn't have given up the sex for seeing all of Europe. Ever. Because sex with Asher is better than anything I ever imagined. I've never felt so in touch with my body. I've never ached to feel someone else's touch so much that I'm in a constant state of pain because I can't have him.

"So, what happens now?" Asher asks as we climb into a taxicab.

I give the cab driver my address.

"What do you mean?"

"I mean, I'm sure you have our whole lives planned out. So, let's hear it. What is your plan?"

I frown. I hate that he thinks I have everything planned out because, honestly, I don't. I know what I want the end result to be. I know what I want from this arrangement. But that's it. I don't know how to get there. I'm just making it up as I go along.

"Well...you move in with me, and we continue on with our married life. We go to work. We make occasional appearances together as a couple. We have sex."

"And how do we decide when this ends?"

I sigh. "When we have had enough."

He nods but doesn't say anything else until we get to my condo. We get out of the taxi.

"I don't know when you need to get back to work or training or whatever you usually do with your time. But I would love for you to go to work with me today or tomorrow to meet everyone. And I can have a moving truck at your place to move whatever you want over to my place today or tomorrow or whenever you would like."

He frowns. "Why are we moving into your place? Why not my place?"

"Because my place is..." I trail off, not wanting to finish that sentence the way I intended.

"Better," he finishes for me.

I nod and blush a little. But I'm not going to apologize because it's the honest truth.

"My place is better than your place. It's bigger. It's more secure. It has furniture that isn't falling apart. It—"

"My place has the beach. It has everything I could ever want," Asher says.

I frown. "My place has a shower that actually shoots out warm water."

"Mine does, too. You just have to wait a little longer for it to warm up."

I throw up my hands. "There is no arguing with you, is there?"

"For however long this arrangement lasts, I just don't want to have to deal with your snobby attitude, thinking you are better than me. Because you're not."

I raise an eyebrow. "I'm not saying that. At least not because I have nicer things and you don't. But I definitely have different morals than you. You think it's okay to steal and cheat while I don't."

"Yes, you're a saint, and I'm the devil. We've already established that." He paces back and forth. "You know what? This isn't worth it. Just file for divorce or an annulment or whatever you need to do to get me out of this mess." Asher starts walking back to the cab.

"Wait," I say, grabbing hold of his arm.

He stops.

"I'm sorry. You're right. I am asking a lot from you to do this. And I appreciate you doing it. How about we come to an arrangement?"

He frowns. "Another arrangement?"

"A deal then? You stay here for a week. Then, I'll stay at your place for a week. Then, we can decide what is best."

He sighs. "Fine, but I expect plenty of sex, no matter which place we stay at."

He walks over and kisses me on the lips, letting enough tongue in to let me know he is ready for sex right now if I'm up for it.

"Oh, I think I can arrange that. But, right now, I need to get changed and ready to go into the office for today. You want to come with me?"

"Sure. If it would help."

I smile. "It would. Come on, let's go get showered and changed, and then I can show you my life."

~

I run a brush through my hair again and then head out of my bathroom in my khaki dress pants and pink blouse. I stop in my tracks when I see Asher in his swim trunks and T-shirt.

"Is that what you are wearing?" I ask.

"Yes. You have a problem with that?"

I shake my head. "Nope." I grab my purse and then head to my door. "Let's go."

Asher grabs hold of my hand. This time, it feels more like he's trying to reassure me that he's with me, which I desperately need because, unlike the honeymoon, as soon as we step foot inside my office building, we are going to be swarmed with questions.

And, sure enough, the second I pull up to the building, we are swarmed with photographers and reporters. I guess it is a big deal when the local girl who runs a large nonprofit almost dies, calls off her wedding, and then marries someone else all in a matter of two days.

I climb out of the driver's seat of my car without even thinking about Asher. I'm sure he's dealt with his fair share of press before. I smile and wave as lights flash all around me. I walk toward the back of my car and wait for Asher to join me. He looks a little shell-shocked, but when he makes it to the back of my car and I grab his hand, his smile lifts.

"You didn't tell me there would be so many people excited to see us, sweetheart," he whispers into my ear.

I laugh. "Just smile and wave until we make it inside where we will get a whole new group of people attacking us."

I start leading him toward my office building as dozens of reporters yell out questions to us.

"When did you get married?"

"Where did you get married?"

"How long have you two known each other?"

"How are you doing after your near-death experience?"

The questions keep coming and coming.

I see Marissa, a reporter who I actually respect, standing near the entrance to the building. She smiles at me and then leans into my ear as I open the door.

"Give me an exclusive, and it will get this mob of people to leave you alone."

I look at her, giving her an I'll-think-about-it look.

She smiles brightly because she thinks I'm going to take her up on her offer. And maybe I will if it will get all the photographers outside to leave us alone.

I take a deep breath once inside. Even though I can already feel the stares on me when we enter the two-story building, I don't care. This is my home. This is where I flourish.

I start walking toward the stairs that lead up to my office, but Asher freezes, holding my hand. I turn and look at him with a fake smile on my face. I shake my head sideways, trying to get him to come on.

He leans down and whispers in my ear, "I've never felt like I should have worn something nicer so much in my life."

I laugh and look at him. He looks like a wrinkled mess. I doubt he even owns an iron. Other than the stubble that covers his face and the tiny lines around his eyes, giving his true age away, he looks like he's eighteen.

"You're fine. Now, come on, or we are never going to make it to my office, and I have work to do." I let go of his hand and start walking toward the stairs.

"Hello, Miss Hart—I mean, Mrs. Calder," my receptionist says from behind her desk.

"It's still Ms. Hart. I'm going to keep my name," I say.

"Of course, Ms. Hart." But Bonnie's eyes don't stay on mine long. Instead, they are eating up Asher.

He must have gotten his confidence back because he is strutting behind me as all the women ogle his body that I know they wish were more visible than what his clothes allow.

I sigh and walk back the five feet to where Asher is now getting swarmed with people asking for his autograph.

"Asher needs to come with me now. But I'll make sure you all have plenty of time later to talk to him and get his autograph," I say a little too sternly.

I grab hold of his hand again, feeling like a mother corralling a two-year-old, which, at the moment, makes me never want kids if it is anything like having to deal with Asher. We make it to the stairs, and I start taking them two at a time, despite my heels.

Even though I live in heels, my work requires me to be quick on my feet. I'm always putting out one fire or another. And I like interacting with the kids who live next door. They've been trying to better their lives after the abuse, neglect, and trouble they got into prevented them from reaching their full potential. I love seeing how resilient the kids are and how they are able to turn their lives around.

"I don't know how you do that in your heels," Asher says when we make it up the stairs.

I smile at him. "Years of practice. I wasn't always so good in heels. I know you won't believe me, but for much of my childhood, I lived in tennis shoes and T-shirts. It wasn't until my early twenties that I started wearing heels and dresses."

"I would have never guessed, but then I've learned to never guess with you."

I keep walking until I get to my office at the back of the building. It's a small room. Not anywhere close to the largest office in the building. But I like it this way. I like having a small office that is just mine. It keeps other people from feeling like they can hang out when I have work to do. Plus, we have plenty of conference rooms that I can go to if I need to meet with more than one person. But there is one awesome benefit to my office that none of the other offices have.

"Holy shit! I thought your condo had a nice view, but this..." Asher says when he walks into my small office.

I take a deep breath, looking at the view. "It was the main reason I chose this building to house our offices."

Asher walks over to the large window that my desk faces. It makes more sense for my desk to face away from the window, but there is no way I could have given up the view.

I take a seat at my desk and fire up my computer. I wait for the endless amount of emails that I get to start pouring in.

"So, what do you want me to do? Besides stare at this incredible view all day," he says.

When I look up, he isn't looking out at the ocean anymore. He is looking at me. I'm the incredible view he is talking about. I blush slightly but am not really that embarrassed.

I glance at my clock. "My mom is going to be here in half an hour. She's excited to meet you. So, it would be great if you could take her to the café downstairs and just get a coffee or something with her."

"Without you?"

I nod. "Most likely. I have a shit-ton of emails I need to answer. And then I need to go over and talk with some of the kids today. I've heard there are a couple who are struggling with the program, and I want to go see to them personally."

His eyes are wide as he looks at me.

"You'll be fine."

"I don't do parents."

I laugh. "Well, my mother isn't really a parent. Technically, I lived with her when I was growing up, but I wouldn't call her a parent. I usually refer to her as Catherine anyway instead of Mother. Especially when I'm at work. So, I really don't care if you impress her or not. Just keep her out of my hair and keep her from drinking anything alcoholic—at least until after lunch."

He sighs. "Fine. But you owe me the dirtiest sex ever on your desk or pressed up against this window after this."

"Well, at least wait until I'm gone for that. Although I would be happy to take you up on that offer if my daughter doesn't," Catherine, my mother, says.

I frown and take a deep breath, trying to calm myself before I get up.

Asher, on the other hand, doesn't bother to apologize for his words, which is one of the things I like about him. He doesn't apologize unless he feels he is actually in the wrong, and it turns out, that isn't very often.

I give my mother a quick hug, like I actually love her and am happy that she is here.

"This is Asher, my husband," I say.

Asher finally stands and extends his hand. "It's nice to meet you, Catherine. I haven't heard much about you, but I'd love it if you would catch me up over some coffee."

Catherine lights up. "I would love to."

I wink at Asher and say a silent, *Thank you.*

He smiles back, conveying that I owe him.

I nod and grin because I actually think he is going to be good at talking with my mother. All he has to do is flash some muscles, and he'll be good.

As they leave, I realize I need one more thing from him.

"What's your schedule for the week, Asher? Do you have any competitions or training that I need to work around?"

"I usually train for at least three hours every morning. After that, I can do whatever for you, sweetheart."

I smile.

Then, my mother grabs hold of his arm, and I know he isn't going to get another word in for the next hour. I turn back to my computer. But at least I can get some work in instead of focusing on my husband who isn't really my husband. I feel myself caring a little too much about him at the moment, but it's nothing a long morning of work can't fix.

After working for almost three hours and getting through most of the urgent emails, all I can think about is Asher.

Shit.

I shouldn't want him. I just had him last night. And, on the plane, we did hand stuff under a blanket. I've gone weeks, months, without sex in the past. *Why am I this needy now?*

Because I never had sex with Asher before. Because I never knew what I was missing before him.

I get up from my desk, stretching. I'm surprised that Asher hasn't texted me that he can't take my mother any longer and I need to come rescue him or that he's calling the whole thing off and asking for a divorce. That's what I would have done if I were him. Nothing is worth having to deal with my mother—or father, for that matter—for this long. It makes me wonder who has murdered whom.

I slip my heels back on that I kicked off while working, and I make my way down to the café where I told Asher to take my mother. I search for five minutes, but I don't see signs of either of them. I walk over to the barista behind the counter.

"Have you seen my husband or mother?" I ask, hoping that she knows who the hell I am. "My husband is a surfer who would be hard to miss, and my mother is dressed like she is going to a ball later today."

The barista smiles. "They were here earlier. Your mother left in a car about an hour ago. And your husband asked for something more fun to do. I sent him across the street to talk with the kids."

I nod. "Thank you."

I run outside into the warm air. I immediately feel drenched in sweat every time I step outside. It makes me wonder why I even bother to wear nice clothes. Maybe Asher has it right. It does make sense to always be wearing swim-type clothing while in Hawaii.

I make it into the building across the street, and thank God for the air conditioner. I'm actually surprised that I didn't see any press waiting for us outside.

But, after I emailed Marissa, she must have kept to her promise to help get rid of the press. I don't know how she managed it. Maybe she allowed them to pick up the piece as well. I don't know.

I run my hand through my hair as I search the home that holds somewhere around a hundred kids on any given day. The age range of the kids varies. But all of the kids here are in need of a fresh start. It's expensive to fly them to Hawaii. But we have found that most of the kids thrive after they come here because it is so different from the environment they were in before. They can actually see a future after coming here. They see the beauty in the world again. So, the money is well worth it.

They come here and heal while we work to find them new

homes. And, with the older ones, we work to get them jobs, college scholarships, or anything else that they need to make it in the real world once they graduate high school. We become their substitute family.

I start walking down the hallway, looking for Asher. I don't have a lot of time to look for him. I need to find the couple of kids on my list and spend the afternoon with them, so I can figure out how to help them. I stop dead in my tracks when I see Asher sitting with one of the teenage boys, playing a basketball video game on the TV. I stand in the doorway and watch them.

"You're kicking my ass, Jordan," Asher says.

"Fuck yeah, I am," Jordan says back.

"Do you cuss like that in front of the ladies?"

Jordan thinks for a minute. "Yeah. But they love it."

"Do they? Then, the chicks must have changed a lot since I was your age. Because most of the women I know don't love it when I cuss. Not the ones I hope to spend more than an afternoon with anyway. If you want a woman you can take out on a date more than once, you are going to have to reduce the amount of cussing. You feel me?" Asher asks.

Jordan nods slowly. "Yeah, I feel you, man. Thanks."

"Now, if you really want to impress a girl, then you should take her surfing."

"But I've never surfed before in my life. I would look like an idiot."

"Well, I can help you with that. An athletic guy like you, I could have you up on a surfboard in no time."

"Really?"

"Absolutely. What does your school schedule look like?"

"I have classes until three and then free time after that."

"I'll come by around three then, and I'll teach you how to surf and how to get that girl to go out with you. But you have to go to classes, or the deal is off. Understand?"

"But why do I need school? I want to play professional baseball. I want to be an athlete. Look at you. You are a surfer. What do you need school for?"

"You don't think I needed an education to do what I do?"

"No, all you do is surf all day and get paid for it."

Asher laughs. "No. It isn't that simple. I don't make a lot of money off of my competition wins. I make most of my money off of sponsors and advertising, which means I have an agent. I spend a lot of my day signing contracts. I have to read contracts and understand them. Otherwise, I'd get screwed out of money that I deserve. I have to be able to protect myself. If not, I don't get to be a surfer anymore," Asher says, looking up at me. Like he knows how stupid it was for him to sign a prenup without actually reading it. But it also says that, above everything else, he trusts me.

"And what is your genius plan if you get injured in your first year? You will need a degree so that you could work as an agent or do something else related to baseball, if that is your passion. But you need education."

Jordan nods and is seriously thinking about everything that Asher said.

"So, do we have a deal? No more skipping classes."

Jordan takes his time but holds out his hand to Asher. "Deal."

Asher shakes it. "Good. Now, get your ass to class."

Jordan smiles, gets up, and then walks past where I'm standing with my arms crossed, leaning against the doorway.

"You married an awesome guy, Mrs. Calder," Jordan says.

"Thank you, Jordan." I consider correcting him, but it seems that everyone is going to start calling me by Asher's last name.

Once Jordan is gone, I walk over to where Asher is sitting on the couch and take a seat next to him.

"How did you just do that?"

"Do what?"

"Jordan is one of our most troubled kids here. I was actually coming over here to talk to him. How did you not only pick him out of all the kids here, but also get him back on track?"

"I don't know if he is back on track or not. It's up to him to decide if he really wants and is ready to be back on the right track. But, hopefully, I gave him a good push."

Asher grabs my legs and drapes them across his body. "And, as far as how I picked him out of all the kids here, I guess I could see a little bit of myself in him."

I cock my head to the side as his lips softly kiss me. Far too soft for what I want. I want passion, the kind where he is going to carry me to the restroom and fuck me.

"What do you mean, you see a little bit of yourself in him?" I ask, genuinely curious now about his childhood. I honestly don't know much about him.

He shakes his head. "I'm not going to spill my guts until you tell me more about you. Because, after spending two hours with your mother, I have a better understanding of how you turned into a wild child. So, tell me a story, and maybe I'll tell you one from my childhood."

I frown. I don't like sharing anything about myself. But I guess it's only fair.

"My parents were never there for me, growing up. They basically left me, and...I mean, they left me to my own devices. They didn't even bother to hire a nanny or cook. I was just on my own. That's why they sent me to Hawaii to live with my grandmother every summer. They didn't want to deal with me, and my grandmother was the one who actually straightened me out. Anyway, my parents would have all of these parties where their fancy friends came over with their fancy jewelry and money. I kind of got good at pickpocketing."

He raises an eyebrow at me.

"I know. I would pickpocket them and take any cash they had. They usually had a couple hundred dollars. But I never spent the money on myself. I would always donate the money or give it to friends who had less money than I did."

"So, you were kind of like Robin Hood? Stole from the rich to give to the poor."

I laugh. "I guess you could say that. I think running this nonprofit kind of became my penance. My parents gave me plenty of inheritance. Enough to comfortably live off of without working another day in my life. So, I live off of that money and don't take a salary from the nonprofit."

He nods.

"Your turn," I say.

"My story isn't really that exciting."

"I don't care. I want to hear it anyway."

He sighs. "Fine. I never knew my mother. She left me when I was still a baby. My father raised me. And, honestly, much of my childhood was amazing. My father was the best. We didn't have a lot of money, but it didn't matter because we loved each other, and we were all either of us needed. But then he died."

"How old?" I ask when Asher stops talking.

"Eleven."

"I'm so sorry."

He shakes his head. "It's okay. It happened a long time ago."

I hold his hand and kiss him on the cheek, hoping that I can somehow take his pain away even though I know I can't.

"I moved from California to Hawaii to live with my coach until I was old enough to live on my own. I didn't realize it then, but he only let me live with him so that he could have a say in my competition and sponsorship earnings. Even though I won a lot and should have had more than enough money to survive on by the time I was sixteen, with him being my legal guardian and signing all the contracts, he got control of my money. I eventually figured it out."

"What did you do?"

"I ran away and lived on my own for a while. I didn't really have a home, so I was couch-surfing for a while. But, after I won one competition, I suddenly had enough money to buy an apartment, and the rest is history."

I tilt his chin up to me and kiss him on the lips, letting him know how much I appreciate him sharing and how much I wish I could take away the pain from his childhood. Within seconds, the kiss turns to more. More kissing, more need, more passion. Asher's hand tangles in my hair, and mine goes under his shirt as Asher pushes me on my back. We make out on the old couch like two horny teenagers.

"Excuse me, Mrs., uh...um..."

We both freeze. We stop kissing. But our hands stay on each other. Because it doesn't matter who is standing in the entryway. We need each other. We are desperate for each other. And, even though he is going to ruin our make-out session, we can at least still cling to each other for a few more seconds.

"You can still call me Ms. Hart," I say with my eyes closed as I press my forehead against Asher's for a little bit longer.

We each suck in a breath, and then I open my eyes back to reality as Asher does the same.

"I have to go," I whisper.

He nods. "I'll meet you back at your place."

I lean forward and kiss his lips one last time. Then, I get up to meet one of my employees who needs me at the door before returning to the hustle and bustle of the office.

"Ms. Hart, I need you to look over some plans, and then I need..." Kenny keeps telling me what he needs as he walks down the hallway, expecting me to follow him so that we can talk and get things accomplished at the same time.

I have to stop though for just a second and look back at Asher one last time before I enter the real world again.

He has a heart. Honestly, I wasn't sure he had one. But it makes my heart ache, just thinking about his.

I turn and hurry to catch up with Kenny. All the time, I'm thinking, *Asher has a heart. And it's a good heart that is capable of love. Who knew?*

My week is almost up, and I can tell that Asher is getting restless at my place. He's accidentally broken a wine glass, a picture frame, and a glass figurine I had sitting on a shelf. It's not that he's clumsy; he's just not used to having so many nice things, and he didn't realize that one wrong movement could cause so much damage.

But Asher has done everything that he was supposed to do. He hasn't complained once about staying in my condo. And, anytime that he was close to complaining, he would just fuck me, and then he'd seemingly like my condo again.

He has spent most of the week at my office other than the few hours a day that he is surfing. He has taken I don't know how many of my kids out for surf lessons.

But he has also spent a lot of time talking with the kids. And, as much as I thought that I should be afraid of what he was telling the kids, I'm not afraid at all. I thought he would tell them that it was okay to drink, party, and do drugs. That it was okay to steal what you needed. But he didn't. He didn't exactly tell the kids that they needed to be models of perfection. He didn't sugarcoat and say that their life was going to be easy. He was completely honest and real with them. He's been doing a better job at connecting with them than many of our counselors have done. I would hire him full-time in a heartbeat if I thought he would say yes and if it wouldn't complicate things further.

Right now, it's a lazy Sunday afternoon. I'm working on my laptop, sitting on my comfortable couch, with my feet stretched out across his lap while he watches some baseball game on the TV. And all I can think about is how I can't imagine how we are going to spend our time at his place. I'm not even sure if his couch can support our weight for this long.

"Why are you staring at me like that?" Asher asks without taking his eyes off the television.

"How do you know I'm looking at you?"

"Because your typing on the computer stopped, and I assume it is because my body has distracted you. I need at least twenty minutes though before I can fuck you."

I laugh. "You're telling me that, if I stripped naked right now, you wouldn't fuck me?"

"Nope," he answers quickly.

"If I wore my black lace lingerie, you wouldn't fuck me?"

"Nope."

I frown. "If I rubbed oil all over my body?"

"Nope."

"If I brought in a model for a three-way?"

"Not even for a three-way. They are way overrated anyway."

I chuckle. "And when did you have a three-way?"

"A couple of years ago. After I won my first international competition. I won half a million in prize money alone. I had my choice of women after that."

I huff. "Why won't you fuck me? Why do you need twenty minutes at least?"

"Because this baseball game is tied, going into the bottom of the ninth, and I want to see who wins."

"I thought you didn't care about watching baseball."

He jumps up and starts yelling at the TV. "Homer! That's a homer. Go, go, go!"

I watch as the ball flies up and then lands in a guy's glove, inches from going over the fence.

"Shit," he says, slowly sitting back down, his eyes still on the TV.

"I thought you didn't care about watching baseball."

He shrugs. "Now, I do."

"And why is that?"

"Well, now that I have a nice TV to watch sports on every day, you've got me hooked to the thing. And there is a kid I'm helping tutor who is a Cubs fan, and I want them to win for once."

"You are tutoring a kid? I didn't know you were smart enough."

He tosses a pillow at me. I catch it with my hands.

"I'm not just a hot body—as much as that is all you use me for."

I roll my eyes. "Don't blame me for your newfound TV addiction."

"I'm definitely blaming you."

"Fine. Then, I'll blame you when I stink because I haven't showered in a week after moving into your place."

That gets his attention. He stares at me like I just spoke Chinese to him or something.

"You're still wanting to move into my place? I thought that was a joke when you said it."

I frown. "It wasn't a joke. I promised that, if you lived here for a week, then I would try out your place for a week without complaining about it. Then, we could make a decision together about where we lived for a while."

He raises an eyebrow. "You are always full of surprises."

He takes my feet back in his lap and begins slowly rubbing them. He might be waiting until the end of the game to fuck me, but I know that I'm at least still in the back of his mind.

He knows that rubbing my feet is one of my biggest turn-ons. I didn't realize it was until this week. I think he is the first guy to ever rub my feet. He did, and I've been putty in his hands ever since. So, I know this is his way of saying that the sex is coming the second the Cubs win or lose this game.

I pick my laptop back up and open it. I never imagined that Asher would be this nice to me. I never imagined that he would actually do anything to help my business. I never imagined I would ever want to do anything nice for him.

But here I am, sitting with my computer, frantically searching for the perfect gift to get him. Something to show him how much I appreciate him. Especially after I found out that his birthday is next week. I thought I would do something small. Take him to dinner or something. But, now, I'm buying him the most expensive gift I have ever bought anyone.

I look up at his grin as he watches the TV.

Damn it. I know this isn't going to end well. For either of us.

"What are you doing?" Asher asks.

I hold the tie out to him.

"I'm not wearing that," he says.

I laugh. "I didn't figure you would, and I don't want you to. Tonight is about celebrating you. Wear whatever you want."

"You're all dressed up though," he says.

I shake my head as I look down at my simple sundress. "I wouldn't call this dressed up."

"It's dressed up to me."

"I'm wearing a dress. That doesn't mean I'm dressed up."

"So, what is with the tie?" he asks.

I walk behind him and place the tie over his eyes. "I have a surprise that I don't want you to see until I'm ready."

I begin tying the tie behind his head, hoping it is enough so that he can't see.

"Do I want to know why you have a tie? It's not mine. Have you been cheating on me?"

I laugh. "Will you relax? You know I haven't been cheating on you. With the amount of sex we've been having lately, I don't think I would have time to cheat on you."

"True."

"I have a couple of outfits that look sexy with a tie. It's mine. It's pink. Not too many men wear bright pink ties."

I check to make sure that he can't see out of the tie by dancing around and acting goofy. When he doesn't respond to my craziness, I smile and grab his hand. "Follow me."

"I can't see. You could be leading me to my death, and I wouldn't know."

I grin. "I could. I guess you will just have to trust me."

I lead him out of my condo and start walking down the hallway to the elevators.

"You're lucky I like fucking you," he says as my older neighbors get off the elevator.

"Good afternoon, Mr. and Mrs. Shayfield," I say as we pass them and walk into the elevator.

"Stop talking dirty, and just do as you're told," I say.

Asher grins. "Fine. But it's my birthday. Aren't you supposed to be doing what I tell you to do? Not the other way around?"

"No. You're supposed to always do what I tell you. We are married, remember?" I joke with him.

He laughs. "Fine. I'll do whatever you want as long as I—"

I put my hand on his mouth, shutting him up, as the doors to the elevator open on the bottom floor. As much as I want to hear him say more dirty, filthy things to me, I want to still be able to live in my building without being completely embarrassed.

I grab his hand and quickly lead him through the lobby of the building and outside.

"Okay, now, I really think you are going to try and kill me. Or push me into the ocean, ruining my only pair of shorts that aren't swim trunks so that I will be forced to wear some suit or something that you have laid out for me upstairs."

I laugh and shake my head. "You are wrong on both accounts."

I keep leading him to my surprise.

"Then, what the hell are we doing?"

"Okay, stop."

He does, just inches from falling off the curb of the sidewalk.

I grimace, hoping he's not going to twist an ankle because of me. I grab his hips and force him to take a step backward.

"Are you ready for your surprise?" I ask excitedly.

He grins. "Ready as I'll ever be."

I pull on one end of the tie covering his head.

"Ow," he says when the tie jerks his head back instead of coming undone, like I expected it to.

I giggle. "Sorry. Here, let me—"

"No. You had your chance." He rips the tie off his eyes.

"Happy birthday!" I shout.

My eyes are glued to him as he looks at the brand-new truck I bought him for his birthday. It's exactly the same as his truck, just completely redone inside and out.

His eyes pop open as he looks at it.

"Well? What do you think?"

"You bought me a truck?" he asks hesitantly.

I laugh. "Yes. I bought you a truck for your birthday. I know you love that old thing that you are always driving around, but I know it's going to die soon. I thought you could use something new to drive that would also remind you of the old one you love so much. Just with a few new features."

"You bought me a truck," he repeats again.

I nod, and then my heart drops. "You don't like it, do you?"

"You bought me a truck."

I shake my head. "I can return it if you don't like it."

He turns to look at me. "You bought me a truck." A grin slowly curls up on his lips.

I bite my own lip, still not sure if he loves it or hates it. I don't know him well enough to know what this reaction means. It isn't how I expected him to react.

"You bought me a truck," he says, now fully grinning.

"If you say that one more time, I'm going to go insane. Yes, I bought you a truck. Do you like it or hate it?"

His arms go around me, and then he's twirling me around. I let out a little squeal, hoping to God this means he's happy with me whether he likes it or not.

"You bought me a freakin' truck! Of course I love it," he says.

He firmly kisses me and then carries me over to the passenger side. He throws the door open and lifts me up into the truck before running to the driver's side and climbing in.

"Holy cow! I thought you just bought me a new truck that was just like mine, but this thing..." He runs his hand over the dashboard that is full of buttons and lights. "This thing has everything."

I smile, but my heartbeat doesn't slow. It's beating on full blast, going about a million miles an hour, as I watch him try out every function of the truck.

"To be honest, I never wanted a new truck. And, when my truck died, I thought I would just buy another old used truck that would last a couple of years and then die. I beat my truck up enough with the sand and heat that I never thought I would want a nice truck."

Shit. He hates it. He thinks it's cool, but he will never use it.

"But, damn, was I wrong. This thing is awesome!"

I grin. "Really? Do you really like it? I can take it back."

He starts the truck and puts it in drive before pulling out onto the main street. I watch as he takes a deep breath of air when he puts down the sunroof to let in the cool ocean air.

"No way am I letting you take this thing back. This thing is awesome. I love it." He leans over and kisses me on the lips. "No one has ever gotten me anything this nice before. I don't care how much you spent on it. I don't care that we aren't really together. I'm not letting you take it back. You bought it and gave it to me. It's mine now."

When he looks at me, his eyes say that I'm his, too. Even though we both know that it isn't true. I'm not his. I can never be his.

"Take a left up here," I say.

"Why?"

I smile. "Because I have one more surprise for you."

He grins. "I like your surprises, Sloane. A lot."

"Good."

I like that, now that I bought him a truck, he will do what-ever I want for the rest of the evening. He knows all I want is to do something nice for his birthday.

He parks the truck in the parking lot by the beach after I give him directions.

"You know I love the beach, Sloane, but I'm starving, and I spent most of the day here. So, it's not really a surprise to take me to the beach."

I shake my head. "You haven't seen the surprise yet. Come on."

I climb out of the truck and wait for him to savor the last few minutes of being inside the truck before climbing out. He finally does.

We automatically link our fingers together, and then I lead him down toward the beach.

When he sees it, he picks me up in his arms and starts kissing me. "Thank God you aren't taking me to a fancy restaurant for dinner."

I laugh. "I know you well enough to know that you don't like eating at fancy restaurants."

"I'm glad I stole you from Wes."

"You didn't steal me. I came willingly."

"Whatever you say, sweetheart. You're mine now. At least, you are tonight."

He finally places me down in one of the chairs and then takes a seat opposite me. The table is simple. It's a white table with white chairs. Nothing over the top. Nothing fancy. I knew he wouldn't want fancy although I did have the chef fix fancy food. I know he isn't opposed to fancy, good food.

The waiter brings over two beers, like I requested. "Would either of you like anything to drink other than beer?"

Asher grins. "Beer is perfect."

"I'll be right back with your first course," the waiter says before disappearing back up to his station several feet away.

Asher cocks his head to one side as he looks at me. "Why are you being so nice to me?"

"It's your birthday. It's, like, a law that you are nice to your husband on his birthday. You might even get lucky tonight," I say, winking.

He takes a sip of his beer. "I know that most wives are nice to their husbands on their birthdays. But we aren't really husband

and wife. More like fake husband and wife. There is no require-ment for fake husbands and wives to be nice. So, why are you?"

"Because I like you, and I want you to be happy. You are kind of growing on me, even if your heart is black."

He chuckles. "You're probably right about my heart, which is why you shouldn't get too close to me. I might just break it."

Too late, I think.

I suck in a breath. It can't be too late. I just have to remind myself how much of a monster he really is. Then, I won't care for him so much.

"Oysters, crab cakes, and calamari," the waiter says, placing a large plate of food in front of us.

We both stare at the appetizer plate. It looks delicious.

"I'll be back with more beers. Anything else you need?"

We both shake our heads.

The waiter leaves again, and we each dig into the food in front of us.

"This is amazing. Where did you order it from?"

I don't answer. I just keep digging into the food and eventu-ally mumble something between bites, a bit ashamed that I ordered it from the nicest and most expensive place on the island. All week, I've been telling him this place has the best food on the island to try and get him to go with me after work one night. But he disagreed. He said anything that cost this much was full of crap and couldn't be the best food on the island. So, I don't want him to find out it's from this place until after dinner is over.

He grins. "It's from Azure, isn't it?"

My cheeks blush, and I nod as my mouth is still full of crab cake. I swallow slowly, waiting for him to argue with me about why I didn't pick a place that I already knew he loved for his birthday.

He takes another bite of calamari. "I hate losing. And I

mean, *hate* losing. But I will concede. This is the best fucking food on the island." He takes another bite of oyster. "No, it's the best food I think I've ever had in the entire world."

I laugh. "I told you, you wouldn't win every time. Not when you're competing against me."

"I win when it's important to win."

His scoots his chair closer to me and then runs his hand up the center of my thigh. I tighten my legs to keep him from inching his hand up further.

"As much as I loved our first romp on the beach, I'm not sure I'm ready for another. Not when José is going to come back any second with more beer and food."

He chuckles and slowly removes his hand. "As much as I want you right now, this might be the first time that I'll be patient enough to finish a meal fully before I fuck you."

"You'll need your strength for sure for what I have planned for you tonight."

"It'd better be fucking. Followed by more fucking. Followed by a short nap and then fucking, fucking, fucking."

I run my tongue across my lip. "There will be no napping, and I think you are missing a fuck or two in there."

José brings us a cooler with beers so that we can grab our own whenever we want. He also brings us each a large steak and lobster even though we aren't even close to finishing our appetizer.

"Eat up. You'll definitely need your strength."

We both eat and chat about work or random thoughts we have. But we mainly just eat in silence as we watch the sun slowly start to set across the ocean while we celebrate Asher.

Somehow, we do manage to finish our plates. And then José brings the birthday cake out.

"I'm sorry. I tried to find out what your favorite dessert was, but I couldn't. So, I had them do a birthday cake at least, and you can order whatever you want for dessert. They have almost everything."

Asher blows out the candle. "I want the cake and you for dessert."

I grin and take my fork to dig into the cake when Asher smears a little of the frosting against my chest.

"We are not fucking on the beach again. I don't care if it is your birthday."

Asher glances up at his truck that is parked just up the beach. "I do know of a very nice place to fuck that is far too clean and could use a little dirtiness."

Asher and I exchange one look, and then we are both running up the beach to his new truck as fast as we can with Asher carrying the cake in his hands. My heart beats fast and not just because I'm running fast.

It does anytime there is a thought of having Asher. I've never needed sex as much as I do when I'm with Asher. I need it almost as much as I need food to eat and air to breathe. It doesn't even make sense to me why I need it with him so much. You would think, with how amazing he is at it, that I would need less to satisfy me, not more. But, every time we fuck, it feels like he hasn't touched me in weeks, months, years.

Asher beats me to the truck and already has the passenger door open for me when I get there. He lifts me up in the truck, so I'm sitting, facing him, and then his lips claim me. We kiss, and it makes me lose my breath. But I don't care. I would survive forever from his lips alone.

Asher slowly climbs up on the truck on top of me until I'm lying back on the front seat bench in his truck. He closes the door behind us, and then we are completely engulfed in our own world. People might be able to make out what we are doing or more likely guess, but they won't be able to really see what we are doing. The windows in this truck are tinted, and we are parked under a tree.

And, even if anyone could tell what we are doing, it doesn't matter. We don't care. We need each other too much to care.

I'm too entranced with his kiss to notice anything. But I feel it when the frosting covers my neck, followed by his tongue licking the sweet sugar off my body.

"I love this cake," he says as he spreads more of the frosting on my body. This time, it's over my breasts before his tongue slowly licks it off.

I moan every time he touches me with his tongue. I tangle my hand in his hair, keeping his tongue against my body. I can't really move. There isn't room in the truck. It's hot in here and getting hotter with every second that passes. I don't care about any of it. All I can focus on is Asher's tongue against my skin.

Asher's hand slides up under my dress and grasps my breast. I arch my back, needing him to touch me more.

"We will have to save this cake for later. I need you now," Asher says.

I feel his fingers run down my body and then slip into my panties. He pulls them down and rubs his thumb across my clit, making me wet in seconds. He slides a condom on before his cock replaces his fingers, and then he's inside me as my back arches, trying to push him in further and further, until he is fully filling me.

I bite my lip, and my toes curl as he thrusts inside me. Our lips touch, and our eyes stay locked as we fuck. I feel words on the tip of my tongue. Words that I never thought I would want to say to Asher. I force the words to stay down. I will not say them. I will not feel them.

I feel my orgasm take over, and it helps to keep down any words or feelings other than complete bliss. I come, and Asher comes as we are locked together.

Asher keeps looking at me after we both have come. His eyes look intense as he looks at me. He opens his mouth to speak but doesn't say anything either.

I hold my breath, waiting to see if he is going to say anything or not. I need him to say it and don't want him to say anything at the same time. Because, if he says anything, then everything will change.

A rattling at the door forces air into my lungs again. Asher pulls out of me and sits up while pulling his pants up. I jerk my dress down and look around for the cause of the noise. Most likely, I'm guessing that it is nothing more than a bird or something that hit his window.

But, by the look of terror on Asher's face, it's much more than just a bird. He stares out the passenger window. I sit up just as Asher rolls down his window.

"Hello, Officer," Asher says to the police officer standing outside the door.

I straighten up in my seat and try to remain calm, but I'm too afraid that the police officer just saw what we were doing and is about to arrest us for indecent exposure.

"Are you the owner of this vehicle?" the officer asks.

"Yes," Asher answers.

"Can I see your license and registration?"

Asher reaches into his pocket and pulls out his license.

"The registration is in the glove compartment," I say.

Asher slowly opens the glove compartment and pulls the papers out. He hands them all to the officer.

He quickly looks at the papers and then says to Asher, "Please step out of the car, sir."

Asher begins to step out of the car.

I stay frozen, not sure what I'm supposed to do.

"Asher Calder, you are under arrest," the officer says as he handcuffs him.

Shit.

I jump out of the truck, not thinking, and run over to them.

"What is he under arrest for?" I ask as I look Asher in his eyes, preparing myself to get arrested next.

"For stealing the truck," the officer says before walking Asher to the back of his cruiser and pushing him inside.

"What? The truck isn't stolen. I was the one who purchased it. It was a birthday gift. If you arrest anyone, it should be me! You have to let him go!"

I look at Asher sitting in the backseat of the cruiser, but he doesn't seem surprised at all to be arrested. In fact, he won't even look at me. He just looks straight ahead.

"Ma'am, I need you to step back," the officer says.

"You have it wrong. You shouldn't arrest him. I'll have him out tonight. You have to let him go."

The police officer shakes his head. "I can't do that. I have a warrant for his arrest. Do you have a way to get home, ma'am? Because I can't let you back inside the vehicle. It's now evidence."

"I'll get home just fine," I say, folding my arms across my chest in frustration.

This doesn't make sense at all. The truck isn't stolen. It must be a mistake or a mix-up.

The police officer climbs into the driver's seat just as two more police cars show up to take possession of the truck they think is stolen. I wrap my arms tighter across my chest, now feeling far too cold for the warm weather that is summer in Hawaii.

"I'm going to get you out tonight!" I shout as the car begins to slowly move away.

Asher looks at me for just a moment. His eyes don't tell me a damn thing. They seem completely empty. Cold. His whole body seems cold. He keeps eye contact with me a second longer, and then the car is too far away for me to see him.

I shiver, feeling completely cold and empty now that he is gone. I pull out my cell phone and arrange for a car to come pick me up. I will keep good on my promise and get everything straightened out tonight. It is all just a big misunderstanding. That's all this is. A misunderstanding.

But I can't shake the feeling that I should have said what I desperately tried to push down when I had the chance. Because, now that he's gone, even if just for a few hours, I regret not saying anything. I regret not telling him my true feelings. Because you never know when you are going to lose someone and never get the chance to say those words.

I shake my head. This isn't good-bye. And I can't say those words, no matter how much I need to.

SEVENTEEN

Sloane

I couldn't get Asher out of jail the night he was arrested. I tried everything in my power, but they wouldn't release him. I had my attorney work on his case, and even he—someone I pay almost a million dollars in salary a year, working for days—couldn't get him out of jail. They claim they have evidence that the truck is the same truck that was reported stolen last week. That with Asher's prior history they won't release him.

It's been a week since his birthday. Since the night he was arrested.

I have spent the week staying at his place. Alone. I slept in his bed. I ate—no, mostly drank beer out of his fridge. I used his outdoor shower and toilet and actually started to enjoy it. I love every part of his shack. I love how simple he lives. And I love his place because it completely reminds me of him.

It took me a while to realize why the police weren't going to just let Asher go. Even if it was truly a mix-up. Even with proof that I was the one who bought the truck for him. That it wasn't stolen. His rap sheet is a million miles long. He has stolen countless cars, jewelry, money. Anything of value, and he stole it. He was in and out of jail most of his adolescence. He was once even charged with an armed robbery that would have put him away for twenty years. It was a miracle he wasn't already in jail.

Although maybe it would have been better if he were in jail. A lot less people would have been hurt if he were in jail this whole time.

I sit in my car outside the jail, waiting for Asher to come out, so I can take him home. It's a strange feeling. I know he didn't steal the truck, but he easily could have. It's been over a year since he was in jail for theft. But he could easily still be stealing and just not getting caught.

Or he could have changed.

I shake my head. He hasn't changed. He stole me. It's no different than stealing a car. Nothing's changed. He's a villain. A monster. I knew that. I just thought that maybe I could be the one to change him. That I could make him different. Better.

My fingers drum against the steering wheel as I wait. My heart beats fast, and my hands are sweaty. I'm nervous, waiting for Asher to come out. Because I'm afraid that one week has somehow changed everything. No, I know it has. I already think of him differently. Just knowing that he has gone to jail for such horrible things makes me feel differently. It reminds me of who he really is instead of the man who knows how to turn me on. How to fuck me and nothing more.

I see the door open and watch Asher walk out. He stops a second when he sees me, seemingly just as surprised to see me sitting in my car as I am at the sight of him. Because, looking at him now, I know that one week can completely change your whole world. One week can change everything.

Asher looks completely different than the man I knew who walked into the building. For one, the clothing he walked into the building with is gone. For some reason, he's wearing shorts and an old-looking sweatshirt that is far too big on him. He starts walking again, and the hood falls down. I gasp in complete shock. His long locks are gone, exchanged for a much shorter cut. His beard has grown out longer than it ever was before. And his eye looks bruised with a cut above it.

He's gone from a relaxed, beach-loving surfer to a hardened criminal overnight. I don't know what happened in there, but gone is the goofy, arrogant smile, and in its place is a menacing grimace. He looks even colder than when the police arrested him.

I'm not sure if he's going to walk to my car or not. He seems mad. I just don't know if he's mad at me, if he thinks I somehow set this all up, or if he is mad at the police and having to spend a week showering in front of other men and feeling afraid for his life at every second.

So, while he is walking down the sidewalk, I take the time to admire his body. I bite my lip as I take in his darker look. A look that I am just as desperate for as his surfer look.

He walks to my passenger door and opens it. He sits down without a word to me. We look at each other, just like we did when he fucked me in the truck, just like we did when he was in the back of the police cruiser. Both of us have so much to say, but neither of us is able to say anything.

I take a deep breath and say, "You hungry?"

He narrows his eyes and nods.

I smile weakly. "I know this great little place that does great American style food just up the road, or I can take you to get something else if you prefer."

He shrugs like he doesn't care.

I pull out of my parking spot and start driving toward the little diner in silence.

When we get to the diner, I stop and look at Asher. "This place makes great milkshakes. I figured we could both use one."

Asher chuckles. "A milkshake would actually be perfect."

I let out the breath I was holding since he stepped foot in my car. I smile. "Good."

We get out of the car, and our fingers brush against each other before Asher finally grabs hold of my hand and gives it a reassuring squeeze. I let out another deep exhale, but I still feel anxious.

We take a seat in one of the booths on the far side of the diner where no one else is sitting. We each order milkshakes and burgers.

"I'm sorry," we say at the same time.

"You have nothing to be sorry for," we say.

Asher relents and lets me speak.

"I'm sorry that you ended up in jail. I didn't realize the police would mistake the truck as a stolen one. I'm sorry your birthday sucked and that I couldn't get you out earlier."

Asher shakes his head. "I'm the one who should apologize. I should have told you the real reason I never have anything nice. Why I haven't replaced my old truck in years even though it's broken down. Why I live in a shack on the beach when I have millions sitting in the bank."

He takes a deep breath as he grimaces and then looks me in the eyes. "It's because I'm a thief. I used to steal cars; now, I steal women's hearts. But the police will always believe that anything nice I own is stolen. You need to know my whole story. It starts ten years ago...

Ten Years Earlier—Asher

I'm not supposed to steal. I know that. I thought I had put the stealing all behind me.

But why is the temptation so great right now?

Maybe because I have had a shitty day. Although that doesn't make what I'm thinking about doing right. But I'm tempted all the same.

I've already done the hard part of sneaking into the garage without getting caught. I watched in my car as the family pulled out of their driveway. Gone for a weeklong vacation. It's not really a challenge. The family leaves the back door that leads into the garage unlocked so that the various people they've hired to take care of the pool and garden have access to their tools. And there isn't anything of value to steal in the garage anyway. They have a second garage for their fancy cars. But the garage is attached to the house.

I doubt they leave the door leading into the house open, but I try it anyway. It's locked, like I suspected. But I know where the spare key is. My friend, Sawyer, had to use the spare key to get into the house when he lost his while he was dog-sitting here last month.

I pull up the floor mat and find the key. I put the key in the door and turn it until it unlocks the door. I push the door open, holding my breath, hoping that they haven't installed an alarm system since I was here with Sawyer. No alarm sounds, so I make my way inside until I'm standing in the family's expansive living room that is two stories high. I can't help but look up at the huge ceiling and large windows that sit uncovered, revealing me to the outside world.

No one can see me, I have to remind myself.

It's dark outside, and I haven't turned any lights on. Man, I'm rusty at this.

I think about stealing one of their fancy cars. That is my favorite thing to steal. I love the thrill of driving out with a fast car that isn't mine. The only problem with stealing a car is getting rid of it before you get caught. I've done it several times in the past, but I've also gotten caught. And I don't plan on going back to jail anytime soon.

I find the stairs in the dark and begin creeping up them. I know enough from my past that, even if I think everyone has gone, it is better to be quiet. You never know if someone has decided to stay behind in the house even if you think they are all gone.

When I make it to the top of the stairs, I'm greeted by a small, fluffy dog that begins jumping at my feet. They left the dog, which means someone is going to be over at some point to let it out. It probably won't be till later since they just left, but to be sure, I have to move quickly.

I walk down the hallway until I find the master bedroom. The door is shut, and even though I'm confident that no one is behind it, I slowly and cautiously open the door.

The little dog decides to join me, still jumping at my feet whenever I walk. I hate dogs for this reason. They are horrible at protecting the home they are supposed to be guarding, no matter the size or breed. And they often just drive me nuts while I'm trying to do my job.

When I'm inside the bedroom, I quickly scan the room, trying to decide what to steal. I know the family is rich and most likely has a safe of some sort somewhere around here along with countless pieces of jewelry. I head toward the closet at the back of the room and find the safe. I'm tempted to break into the safe. The best items are in the safe. But the safe is the worst place to steal from. They know exactly what they have in the safe. The items they are less worried about, they keep in the bathroom or bedroom, and those are easier to steal without them noticing.

That's my target. Items that they won't even notice missing. So, as much as the safe calls my name, as much as I want to crack it because I can, I won't.

I turn my attention toward the bathroom and find the jewelry box sitting on top of the counter. I'm wearing gloves, so I don't have to worry about leaving my fingerprints behind. I open the box and slowly move the jewelry around, trying to find something valuable that doesn't look like it has been worn in a while. When I get to the back of the box, I find two necklaces in the same container.

I grin. This is exactly what I want. If I take one of the necklaces, it won't even look like anything is missing. I take the diamond necklace out and stare at it. It's not the most expensive thing in this house or even in the jewelry box. But the necklace is easily worth twenty thousand to thirty thousand dollars. It's enough to satisfy my urge to steal.

I place the necklace into my pocket. Then, I close the jewelry box and put everything back in its place. I start looking to see if there are other items in the bathroom or bedroom that are worth stealing when I hear the distant sound of sirens.

Shit. I glance around the room more thoroughly and see motion detectors in the corner of the room.

Shit. Shit. Shit. I must have triggered a silent alarm when I entered the house.

I start running down the stairs in the dark. The yipping dog is still jumping at my feet. I run fast enough that the dog can no longer keep up.

I make my way to the back door and open it. I move into the garage. The police sirens grow closer with every second that passes. I have to make a run for it. My car is parked a street back, so I begin running through the backyard to take the most direct route even though it's risky. The fence at the back is high and hard to climb, and any number of neighbors could see me and report me.

I run as fast as I can as I turn and look over my shoulder. I see the police cars arriving at the house. I dart behind a large tree as flashlights shine into the backyard. I take several deep breaths while I wait for my chance to jump the fence and disappear into the darkness.

If I admit it to myself, I love the excitement of the police being here. I love how my heart is racing. I love the thrill of getting caught. I just don't like actually getting caught.

The lights turn away from me and move toward the other half of the yard. I take one more deep breath before I run toward the fence that is ten feet or so in front of me. There is no turning back now. No place to hide. I have to make it over the fence that towers over me as quickly as possible before they decide to shine their flashlights back in my direction.

I reach the fence as beads of sweat pour off my neck. I run, jump, and grab hold of the large tree branch that is hanging over the fence from the neighbor's yard. I begin using my arms and legs to climb over the wooden fence.

I finally reach the top and throw my legs over before jumping down. I'm not safe just because I'm on the other side. In fact, I will never be safe again. I will always be on the run. Always on alert that I could be caught.

I begin running through the neighbor's yard. I trip and almost fall over a tree branch that I didn't see in the dark, but I keep running. I run until I reach the neighbor's gate. I carefully open it, hopeful that it doesn't squeak or make a sound, and then I make it through. I quickly shut it, and then I'm in the clear. It's a straight shot to my car.

I don't run now that I'm in clear view of the neighbors. Instead, I walk as calmly as I can toward my car. I quickly start it up and then drive at a normal speed, away from the area.

I stole again. I'm a thief. I don't even care about the money or things that I steal. I live for the rush I just experienced. I just don't know how to get this feeling without stealing. If I could find a way, I would never look back at this lifestyle again.

~

Five Years Earlier—Asher

My heart is racing. It always does on a night like this. The sun is just beginning to set. Before it rises again in the morning, I'm going to have a sweet-ass new car, and I'll be halfway to Mexico where I will sell it and then do it all over again.

I put my headphones on and then flip the hood of my sweatshirt up while I sit on the bench outside the dealership, waiting for the rest of the straggling employees to leave. The music is loud and steady. I try to use it to steady my heart, but I know that nothing is going to be able to do that. Not until I have the car in my possession, and I'm long gone.

So I sit and wait, hiding my face beneath the shadows of the hood. If employees drive by the bench, they will just think I'm waiting for the bus. They won't remember me. They never do. The few times I was caught were because I had been speeding after I stole the car or had friends who ratted me out. Neither is a mistake that I will repeat again.

I watch the last employee leave for the night, which leaves me exactly one hour until the janitor comes to clean. It's not quite dark, but it's dark enough to not draw too much attention to myself. I wait two more songs to ensure that no one is coming back because they forgot something inside, and then I get up, avoiding eye contact with the woman who just sat down on the bench next to me.

I walk slowly and carefully with my head down, making sure to avoid my face being caught on the security cameras that circle the outside of the dealership. I reach the door and then put on gloves before pulling out a lock pick. I enter the code I already gathered into the alarm system to prevent the alarm from going off and use the pick to unlock the door.

The door lock is loose and is easy to pick. It practically pops open on its own. I push the door, careful to keep my head down. Even though the alarm system is down, the cameras are still fully operational. So, I have to ensure that my head remains down to keep them from learning my identity. To stay out of jail.

I walk straight to the Lamborghini that is sitting in the middle of the showroom. The keys are, of course, not in it. I could spend minutes that I don't have searching for the keys, or I could hot-wire it. I go for option two.

I hot-wire the car, and then I get ready for the part that really gets my heart racing. The part that I live for. I stomp on the gas, going full speed ahead. I slam through the glass and drive as fast as I can away from the dealership.

I stole the car even though I don't need the money. Even though I don't need the car. Just because I want the freedom to feel how I do right now. I just want to live.

～

Present—Sloane

Asher finishes his story. "That's why I'm dressed the way I am. That's why I cut my hair off. I'm never going to be just a surfer. I'm always going to be part thief, no matter that I don't actually steal cars anymore. That is what the police think of me. I'm a thief.

"You knew that I was trying to steal you from Wes. But you don't treat me like I'm the monster that I am. You act like I'm just a normal person. You need to know that this is who I am. I'm a thief. This is me."

I nod, trying to take in what he said. "I know you are a thief. I've always known. Now, I just know how much of a thief you really are. But it doesn't matter. We aren't really married. Not in the way that counts. I've kept the story out of the news. I've just been telling everyone you were sick with the flu this week. No one knows where you really were."

He shakes his head. "You don't understand why it matters

that you understand me. That you understand that I steal because I have to. I need that rush. I need that adrenaline boost that nothing else gives me. I need to feel alive. I need to fill a void that has never properly been filled. And stealing often does that for me."

He lifts my chin up to make sure I'm looking at him. "But I need you to know that I need you more." He hesitates a second and then says the thing that both of us have been avoiding for days, "I love you, Sloane."

EIGHTEEN

Sloane

"*I love you.*"

Three simple words with so much meaning.

He said them. I never expected that he was capable of love. That he would be able to love. But here he is, saying it, and I believe every word that fell from his lips. I know that he loves me. I've felt it for far too long now. We have both been avoiding it. But, now that it has been said, I wish he would take it back.

Every woman wishes for this moment when her boyfriend tells her that he loves her. I should be happy, over the moon, to realize that this arrangement has turned into something real. It has turned into something more than even I could have imagined.

But I'm not happy. I'm devastated. Because I now know what comes next, and I can't bear for it to happen.

"You don't have to say it back. In fact, I don't want you to say it until you feel it, too. I'll wait. I'm patient. I just want you to know that I want more. More than this arrangement that we originally set up. Because time in jail has taught me one very important thing. That I don't want to live without you. I know that I have to change. I have to be a better person, but being with you makes me that way. Being with you makes me want to believe that love can not only exist, but also last. I never thought that before."

I open my mouth to speak, but Asher continues, "When my father died, I was a mess. I hated that I loved him because the pain of losing him was too much to bear."

"How did he die?"

"He was shot."

"I'm so sorry," I say, wanting to know more because it's clear that he has more to say on the subject.

But he doesn't.

"I love you. Our pasts no longer matter. What matters is, if we have a real future together or not. What matters is, if you love me, too. Or if you could ever love me. If you could ever forgive me for what I've done."

I open my mouth to speak, but he beats me to it. "They are really taking forever with our milkshakes, huh? I should flag our waiter down and—"

"Will you shut up?" I say, laughing nervously.

Asher finally stops talking.

"I love you, Asher. I've felt it since the night of your birthday. I just pushed down the feeling because I thought we couldn't be together. We couldn't love each other. That wasn't the arrangement. The arrangement was to help each other. Nothing more. But I do love you."

Asher grins, and it is the brightest grin I've seen on him since I picked him up from jail.

"You love me?"

I smile because his grin is infectious. Even if I know that this is the start of our end, I still enjoy this moment with him. We love each other. No matter what happens after, this is a happy moment.

"I love you."

Asher reaches across the booth and kisses me on the lips.

"Here are your milkshakes and burgers."

"Can we get them to go?" we say at the same time.

We grin again.

"I'll be right back," the waiter says.

I dig out some cash and throw it on the table to cover our meals that aren't going to be eaten until later. We stand up and grab the to-go boxes, and then we practically run to my car. We jump in, and I step on the gas as soon as I can and peel out of the parking lot.

Tonight might be our last night together before everything changes, and I plan on making every minute count.

I speed back toward our home. I push that thought right out of my head. It's not our home. It's his home. It will never be ours.

Asher starts kissing my neck as I drive. With every kiss, I can feel it all over my body. Every nerve in my body is on fire, begging to be touched and kissed.

"You'd better stop that, or we aren't going to make it back to your place. And, last time we did it in a car, it didn't turn out so well in the end," I joke.

Asher stops kissing my neck for a second and has a solemn look on his face.

"I'm sorry. Too soon?"

He shakes his head and then kisses me again on the neck to show that it isn't too soon. "Why aren't we going back to your place?"

I swallow, trying to calm my breathing that is much too fast. "Because I fell in love with your place while you were gone."

A slow grin returns to his face as he sits back, staring at me. "You've been staying at my place while I was gone?"

I nod.

"I think I just fell even more in love with you, if that's possible."

I open my mouth to speak, but he kisses my neck again, and a moan comes out instead. All of my thoughts disappear. I try to focus on driving back to his place, but my attention is definitely on his soft lips that caress every inch of my neck.

I don't know how I make it back to his place, but somehow, I do. I jump out of the car, already knowing the perfect place that I want him to fuck me. I start running, and he chases me. He likes the thrill of the chase; I know that much.

And, now that he has me, now that he doesn't have to chase me anymore, will I be enough?

But I don't have to worry about that. Right now, I run until I find a secluded spot where the ocean tide is high.

Asher catches up to me and grabs me from behind, wrapping his arms around me. He kisses me again and again. He stops with his arms around me, and we look out at the sun over the ocean.

"Come inside. I want you in my bed."

I shake my head. "No. The beach is our place. I want you here."

He chuckles. "I'm not fucking you against the sand again."

"I'm not asking you to." I look down at the ocean in front of us.

I don't wait for him to give me all the reasons that the ocean is just as bad or worse of a place to fuck than the sand. I'm sure it is, but I've never fucked in the ocean before. And, even if it isn't perfect, it is what we both need.

Because, as much as he now looks like a thief, I need him to look like Asher again. The man I fell in love with, who has a heart. Who cares about other people, about me. Who loves me.

I grab his hand and lead him into the ocean until we are both waist-deep and covered with water.

"I need Asher tonight. The man I fell in love with, not the thief," I say.

"I can be whatever you want, Sloane. I wanted you to be mine, but instead, I'm yours."

I smile weakly and then stare at the sweatshirt that is covering his chest and body. Clothes that make him look so much like a thief instead of the man I fell in love with. I grab hold of the zipper and slowly lower it. His hard chest and abs come into view. I remove the sweatshirt and then hand it to Asher, who curiously looks at me.

"Throw it out into the ocean," I say.

He frowns. "You know this is littering."

I sigh. "Just do it. You need to let your past go."

He takes the sweatshirt and wads it up in a ball. Then, he throws it as hard as he can out into the ocean. We both stand for a moment, looking at it as it disappears beneath a wave.

When we look at each other, I jump into Asher's strong arms, and he carries me out further into the ocean. I grab on to his short hair that I know will eventually grow back into the long waves, and I wrap my legs around his waist. He rubs his hands up my thighs under the light sundress I'm wearing until he is grabbing my ass.

He kisses me, showing me how much he is mine. He pulls my lip into his mouth while I move my hand up and down his neck, grabbing hard, needing him desperately. He stops walking when we are both about chest-deep in the water.

He pulls our lips apart, just far enough that he can look me in the eye. I think he is going to say something serious about why he loves me or wants me.

"I don't have a condom," he says.

I laugh but realize that I don't have a condom either. I think he expects me to pull one out of my bra again or something.

"I don't have one either." I frown.

Asher takes a deep breath as we both realize that we are going to have to wait—at least until we can find one inside or go grab one at the store.

"I'm on the pill," I say out of nowhere. I don't know why I said it. Like the pill is magically going to fix our predicament.

"I'm clean. Although I don't expect you to trust me."

"I'm clean, too. And I do trust you."

We each take a deep breath in and out and then decide to trust each other even though I have no reason to trust him, and he doesn't know me well enough to trust me. Even though he thinks he does.

He thinks I'm perfect, incapable of doing anything wrong. He's wrong. I'm more than capable of ripping out his heart. But he trusts me. And, at least tonight, I don't plan on betraying that trust.

We kiss again, slower this time, as the waves crash around us. I reach for his pants, pushing them down so that I can feel his cock against my stomach. He lifts me up and gives me one last chance to back down before guiding me onto his cock.

I float in the water as Asher guides me up and down, our lips locked and my hands grasping on to his shoulders.

Maybe other people have had bad experiences of fucking in the water. But this is different than anything I've ever experienced. The ocean is the perfect place for us. We both understand it; we get it. The waves crash in, moving Asher in and out of me. I ride him over and over as the waves and Asher move me.

I feel freer than I have felt in a long time, fucking like this. But, when I look into Asher's eyes, I realize why this feels so much different than any other experience I have ever felt before. Because, this time, we aren't fucking.

"I love you," Asher whispers against my lips.

I can barely catch my breath, but somehow, I manage to say back to him, "I love you, too."

This time is different. It's making love, not fucking.

And, if I could take this moment with me forever, I would. Just live right here on the beach in Asher's arms and never return to the real world. The problem is, when the sun sets and this moment is gone, everything will be different. Because I know what I have to do next, and it's going to change everything.

NINETEEN

Asher

She said, "I love you."

That was music to my ears.

But I can't help but think, *What the fuck is wrong with me?*

I've thought it every day for the last week.

What the fuck is wrong with me?

I don't fall in love with women. I've seen the heartache that comes when that happens. Someone always gets hurt.

But, with Sloane, everything is different. I've fallen in love with her. I want her to be mine forever. I just have to make it official.

I know she loves me. Even before she said the words, I knew it was what she felt. But something has been holding her back. Something has been preventing her from moving forward. From actually letting herself be in love with me.

She let herself just be in the moment for one night. That one night when she said she loved me. But, the rest of the week, she has kept her distance. She's been busy at work. I don't know why though.

Is she upset she found out that I'm a thief, a criminal who has been in and out of jail too many times to count?

Is she upset that she fell in love with me?

Is she not convinced that I'm in love with her?

Does she think our lives are too different for us to be together?

Whatever the reason, I'm going to fix it tonight.

I haven't told her why I started stealing yet. She probably thinks I was just a crazy, wild child who liked hurting people. And, while that is part of the excitement for me, it's not the whole story. Not even close. I have to explain everything to her.

Sloane is working late again tonight, which gives me plenty of time to set everything up. I sling the bag filled with roses and flowers over my shoulder. I want tonight to be perfect for her. I'll start with decorating her bedroom. I figure we will stay at her place tonight since it's much nicer than mine. Tomorrow, I hope we can start searching for a new place together. Or maybe we will always split time between my place and hers.

I don't give a damn where we live. I just want her.

I have more decorations in the truck she bought me. I'm going to use them to decorate the beach later. I know it's cheesy to propose on the beach, but it's our place. Sloane won't care that it is cheesy. She will care that I put effort in. She will care that I love her. That's the only thing that is important.

But, still, I have no idea if she will say yes. I think most men who propose already know what the answer is going to be when they ask the question. They have already talked to their girlfriends about it. They might have even picked out a ring together, and then they go through the motions of proposing.

Sloane has no idea I'm about to propose. No man would propose so soon. But no man would have gotten himself in this predicament anyway. Fake married to a woman after he stole her from her fiancé, only to later fall in love with said woman. It's a crazy story that is only found in romance books but not in real life.

So, when I propose to Sloane, it has to be big. I'm going all out with decorations, music, champagne—the whole bit. I'm being the most romantic I can be.

But, first, I'm going to tell her everything. I don't want her to say yes without knowing fucking everything.

I walk over to the elevator where Archie, the elevator operator and security guard, greets me.

"Hello, Mr. Calder. How are you doing today? Here to see Ms. Hart?"

"I'm doing very well. I have a nice surprise tonight planned for Sloane. So, don't ruin it for me."

"I'm very happy to hear it. Ms. Hart has seemed very preoccupied and stressed lately. Hopefully, you'll be able to cheer her up."

I frown and nod as I step into the elevator. Even Archie has noticed that Sloane is unhappy. *Maybe I missed something else that has been going on. Maybe I should wait a little longer to propose.*

I feel the box that the ring is in burning a hole in my suit pocket. I can't wait to propose.

For one, as soon as Sloane sees me in this suit, she is going to know something is up. I'm wearing a suit, so she will know that I have changed. That I'm not just a thief or a surfer. I'm a man desperately in love with her, who will do anything for her. Including buying and wearing a useless suit.

The elevator doors open, and I step out and walk over to her door. I dig in my pocket and realize I forgot the keys to her place. I never lock my place, so I usually leave my keys in the truck. I know, if someone really wants to steal it, it won't matter if the keys are in it or not. I hate using my skills to break in her door today, but I'm not going all the way back to my place to get the keys to her place. I'm on a tight schedule because, at anytime,

Sloane could call me and tell me that she's leaving work and ready to go out to dinner. That's all I've told her. That I'm taking her out for dinner. It is a Friday night after all.

I'll just pick her up and get her to change into a nice dress. I know her well enough to know that she has plenty of nice dresses hanging in her closet.

I pick the lock on the door and enter her condo. I take a deep breath as I always do when I enter her condo. It smells like clean linen. It's Sloane's smell. Clean and perfect, just like her.

I'm sure she has her faults, but these last few weeks, I haven't found any. She's perfect. Intelligent, sassy, caring, and beautiful. She's everything I never knew I wanted.

The linen scent that is Sloane is covering the condo. It smells stronger than usual, like she was recently here even though I know she's been in her office all day long. I could just stand here and smell her all day, but I have to work fast.

So, I start walking to her bedroom when I hear soft music playing. I shake my head. Her alarm clock plays music like that. She must have forgotten to turn it off when she left for work this morning. She stayed in bed while I got up to go surfing this morning, like usual.

I open the door and freeze.

I feel like I've just been stabbed in the heart.

Shot.

Broken.

And left for dead.

I can't move.

I can't breathe.

And I'm sure that my heart has stopped beating.

I close my eyes, hoping that this is a nightmare. That, at any second, I'm going to wake up and realize that what I'm seeing isn't really happening.

But, when I open my eyes, she's still there, lying naked, in her bed with another man.

It has to be a mistake.

She's perfect.

She loves me.

She would never hurt me like this.

Never.

I take a breath, finally able to breathe, when I realize that it is some sort of mistake. She has to have an explanation for what is happening.

"Sloane, what's going on?" I ask like I'm not witnessing what I am.

"I'm sorry," she says with tears in her eyes.

Two words.

"I'm sorry."

They tell me everything I need to know.

She cheated on me.

She broke my heart.

She made me believe in love and then destroyed me.

I'll never recover from this.

I know that.

I loved her more than I loved stealing.

I loved her more than I loved surfing.

I loved her more than I loved breathing.

But she didn't love me back.

Or, if she did, she was too scared to just be in love with me.

She had to ruin any chance that we had.

My initial gut reaction is to walk over and punch the naked man in the face. He deserves it.

But then, when women slept with me, I never thought I was the reason for them to have strayed. Well, at least, not the full reason.

People aren't supposed to get married. Everlasting love doesn't exist.

I knew that.

But I let myself fall in love with Sloane anyway.

I want to hate her. Yell at her. Do something to show her how angry I am with her.

But I'm not really angry. At least, not with her.

I'm angry with myself.

Love doesn't exist. And, when it does, it's selfish love that only lasts until that person falls in love again—with someone else.

So, as much as I want to yell at Sloane, ask her why, try to understand her, try to forgive her...

I can't do any of those things.

All I can do is turn around and walk back out the door, pretending like life didn't just fuck me over again. Like the only woman I've ever loved didn't just steal my heart and then destroy it.

TWENTY

Asher

I hold out my shot glass. "Another."

Paige smiles sweetly. "I'll just leave the bottle here for you guys. Don't tell anyone."

Luca takes the bottle and pours me another one. "I hate to say this, but I told you so."

I glare at Luca as I lift the glass of tequila to my lips and pour the shot down my throat. I've lost track of how many shots I've done. I don't care anymore. I need something to numb the pain. And tequila is that something.

"Say it all you want. I need to hear it. I should have listened to you."

Luca laughs. "You shouldn't ever listen to me. You know that."

Luca looks down at the prenup contract. "You also shouldn't sign anything without talking to a lawyer first. You do understand that you are an idiot for signing this."

"I don't care."

"You are going to care when she takes everything you own. Your house, your money, your trucks—everything is now hers."

I shrug. "Let her have it. I don't want it."

Luca shakes his head. "You aren't sleeping on my couch when you have nowhere else to go."

"I'll make more money. I only get one heart, and it's gone now."

He shakes his head at me. "I don't know what you have turned into, but you are one giant mess, man. She's really fucked you up. You know that, right?"

I dump more of the tequila into the shot glass and take a drink. I don't care anymore. I have lost everything I cared about. All I want now is to spend the rest of my life here, at this bar, drinking. I no longer have a home. That's now hers. I no longer have either trucks. They are now hers. I can't go back to the beach, to the ocean. Everything I ever owned or loved is now hers.

"You need to leave this bar, man. It's been two weeks since the divorce was finalized. You weren't even married for real. You thought you were in love, but you can't fall in love with a chick that fast. You have to get over her. There are plenty of other fish in the sea, and if you got out of here and started training, you could actually earn some money and buy yourself another shack on the beach instead of sleeping outside a bar every night," Luca says.

I lay my head down on my folded arms on the table as I stare at the empty shot glass. After I puked about a week ago, Paige implemented a new rule where I can only have one shot every half hour. It doesn't matter though anyway. The pain is always here now. The alcohol is no longer strong enough to take the pain away.

Luca sighs. "Well, cheer up. I have great news for you."

My eyes dart up to him and then back to the glass in front of me. There is no way he has great news.

"I'm going to introduce you to my girlfriend. You can play your silly games on her. You can try to steal her and fuck her and do whatever you do to cheer yourself up."

"Get rid of your girlfriend yourself, Luca. I'm not going to do it for you."

Luca sighs again. "You really have to get over this girl. This isn't healthy. Have you even talked to her since she cheated on you?"

I shake my head.

"You need closure. Go talk to her. Yell at her. Whatever you need to do. Then, move on." Luca grabs my arm and lifts me out of my chair. "You are going to go talk to her. Now."

He walks me out of the building. "How much have you had to drink?" he asks.

"Not enough," I say.

Luca studies my eyes and then confirms that I haven't really been drinking. Not since Paige implemented her new rule. I've had maybe two drinks today since I also know, every other shot, she just fills with water, hoping I won't notice. I noticed though.

He reaches in his pocket and then flips me the keys to his car. "Go get closure. Get revenge. Get even. Apologize. Whatever you fucking need, go get it."

I started at her office, but she wasn't there. I talked to her receptionist, who said she hadn't been in, in weeks. Probably off fucking her new beau. I should warn him that she's going to do the same thing she did to me to him. Fuck him, make him fall in love, and then rip out his heart.

I thought I was a monster. But she's just as bad. No, she's worse.

Because I tell people up front who I am. And, if they let me into their life, that is their problem. She pretends to be an angel for those less fortunate. She protects kids and gives them the help they need. But then she goes and hurts men without a second thought.

I tried her condo, but Archie wouldn't let me up to see her. He looked sad when he talked to me. I finally got him to tell me that she wasn't there, and her missing car from the parking lot confirmed it.

When I exited her building, I was swarmed with reporters. I ignored them all. I shouldn't have. I should have told them the real reason for our divorce. That she cheated. Not the crap that she has been feeding them about a whirlwind romance that ended because we were too different and we realized our love would never last. That we were just together to help each other through a difficult time. I should leak the prenup agreement that she had me sign that caused me to fucking lose everything. Then, we will see whose side the media is on.

I can't do that to her though, as much as I want revenge. I want her to feel exactly how I feel right now, but I can't. I just can't bring myself to do it. I can't bring myself to hurt her like that. Because, for reasons I will never understand, I still love her.

And, if she did one thing for me, she helped me realize that, even though I don't believe in lasting love, I shouldn't destroy it for those who do. Because, just maybe, if a couple has a fighting chance to last forever, then they actually will.

Even if they don't, I know I will never get the same thrill out of breaking a couple up again. Because every time I tried, I would be brought back to this feeling. This desperate, angry, sad feeling that I will never be able to escape from again because of her. But, for some stupid fucking reason, it makes me want to try again. Find some woman who can actually love me. That I could feel that way blows my mind the most.

I jump back in the car and start driving. First, I need closure. That is what Luca said. And, for once, I believe him. He's been in enough relationships to know that, that is what I need right now.

I don't know where else to look for her. I'm guessing that she's in that asshole's bed. But I have no idea where he lives, and that isn't the best place to get closure. All I would end up doing is getting in a fight that could land me back in jail.

So, I just drive. I guess I'll eventually go back to her place and see if she ever shows up. But, for now, I drive. I drive to our place on the beach and stop Luca's car. Maybe this is a way to get closure without actually having to speak to her. Maybe, if I tell the world how I'm feeling here, in our place, it will be enough that I can figure out how to move on.

I get out of the car, and a cold draft of wind blows, sending a shiver through my body. It doesn't really ever get cold here. Not enough to need anything but an occasional rain jacket. But that wind felt different. It felt cold, chilling.

I smile weakly. At least Hawaii still gets me. Still understands me and supports me. I just have to convince myself to get my ass back out into the ocean again.

I walk down the beach before I spot her blonde hair blowing in the wind. She has a light sweater wrapped around her shoulders as she sits on the beach, looking out at the storm that seems to be rolling in over the ocean.

I stop for a second. I could turn around, and she would never know that I was here.

Pussy, I think. *Just go talk to her. Get closure.*

I'll go pick up a six-pack of beer on my way back to Luca and drink the night away. But, first, I have to go talk to her.

I walk to where she is sitting and sit down next to her without a word. She doesn't glance over at me. She just tightens her grip on her sweater, and I know that she knows it is me sitting next to her.

I sit there, just staring out at the ocean with her, trying to figure out what I need from her. What I need to get over her. I don't have a clue. But the longer I sit next to her, the clearer what I need becomes.

I reach out and softly touch her chin to get her to look at me. She flinches at my touch.

I pull my hand back and wait for her to look at me. "Why?"

TWENTY-ONE

Sloane

He asked, "Why?"

That's the first word I've heard him say since that night. That's all he gave me. One word.

No context about how he is feeling. Although I can tell, from the pain that is apparent on his face, the alcohol on his breath, and the brokenness of his body, I hurt him. More than I even thought I would.

I hurt Asher.

Ruined him.

Destroyed him.

And all he wants to know now is why.

I don't have to tell him. In fact, I thought I never would. But I think the story needs to be told. He needs to understand why. Then, maybe all can be forgiven. *Both* of us can be forgiven.

~

One Year Earlier

I hear the door to my condo slam as my roommate and best friend in the whole wide world walks in.

"Did you pick up groceries?" I ask from my spot on the couch. I don't know why I ask. I already know that she didn't pick up any groceries.

"Oh, Sloane, I just met the most amazing man!" Danielle says, flopping onto the couch.

I sit up, panicked now. "What do you mean, met? Like, as a friend? You're engaged, Danielle. You don't meet new men."

"Yeah, like a friend. Of course I didn't mean, like a boyfriend. I'm engaged to the most amazing man. But this guy, I could talk to him for hours. He just gets me. You know? I think he might be gay, or I would hook him up with you."

"I'm happily dating Wes," I say.

"No, you're boringly dating Wes. That guy is a complete bore. You need to find someone better. Hotter. This guy is hot. Did I tell you that?"

"No, but you shouldn't be determining how hot other guys are. You are engaged to Wade. Wade should be the hottest guy in your world."

Danielle rolls her eyes. "Of course Wade is the hottest guy in my world. But this guy, he's dreamy. But, like I said, I'm pretty sure he's gay."

"How sure?"

She shrugs and then skips off to her bedroom across from mine.

"Danielle, it's your turn to get groceries this week!" I shout from the couch.

But it's too late. Danielle already has her music turned way up, and I know she won't be coming back out for hours. I sigh and grab my keys to head to the grocery store. I really don't understand why I even bother with a roommate.

I open the door and smile. Sitting on our doorstep are three boxes filled with groceries.

I laugh. Danielle might never do things the same way as me or any other normal person would, but at least she gets things done.

~

I open the door to my condo and start walking toward my bathroom. I'm exhausted, and I need a hot shower to help me relax.

The hall bathroom door opens, and I step back as my mouth falls open.

A naked man steps out. Well, naked, except for the tiny towel wrapped around his waist. When he sees me staring, he rips the towel off and throws it over his shoulder as he walks past me and to Danielle's room. He gives me a little wink first and then disappears into her bedroom.

"Danielle!" I yell at the top of my lungs.

Danielle comes running out of her bedroom. "What's going on? I didn't leave the toaster on again, did I? I promise, I didn't mean to."

I sigh. Living with Danielle is like raising a little sister. "No, you didn't almost burn down our condo again. No, you did something far worse than that," I say, scowling at her.

"What?" she says, still not getting it.

"What is a half-naked man who isn't your fiancé doing in our condo?"

"Oh. That's Asher. He needed a place to shower after he was finished surfing. I let him come up here to use ours since we live so close to him."

"Asher, the gay guy?"

"Technically, he's not gay," Danielle says, not meeting my eyes.

"What do you mean, technically? He either is or isn't."

"That's not true. There are plenty of bi people in the world, you know."

I frown. "Is he one of those people?"

"No."

"Then, what is he doing in our condo?" I hiss.

"He's a friend."

"A friend you need to get rid of ASAP if you still want to get married next week."

She rolls her eyes. "I'm still getting married next week. He's just a good friend."

"Get rid of him."

Danielle huffs and then walks back into her room without saying another word to me. I doubt she talks to me for a few days. That's her usual way of dealing with a fight. She doesn't speak to me for days. She's still very much a child. But I'm not ready to be a mother yet. Well, not to any more kids than I already am a makeshift mother to.

I sit down on my couch with a bowl of popcorn and a glass of wine. I have a chick flick ready to go. I just got back from Danielle's rehearsal dinner, and I just want to sit here and relax before the chaos of tomorrow starts.

And I remind myself that it is okay that I'm not even close to getting married. Wes is nice, but he's not the kind of guy I want to marry. Even he knows that.

Danielle bursts through the door just as I'm about to press play on the video.

"What are you doing here? I thought you were staying in a suite at the hotel tonight."

"I was," she says through sobs.

I put the bowl of popcorn down as I look up at Danielle, who is soaking wet and sobbing.

"Sweetie, what is wrong?" I ask, getting up and running over to her. "Did Wade do something? Is there something wrong with the wedding? What's wrong?"

She shakes her head and walks over to the couch. I sit next to her, and she collapses into my lap. My arms automatically go around her.

"Whatever it is, I'm sure things will be better in the morning."

"No, they won't."

"Talk to me then. Tell me what is going on."

"I slept with him."

"Who?"

"Asher. And then he dumped me after."

"What do you mean? What about Wade?"

"I broke up with him before I slept with Asher. The wedding is off. There is no way he will take me back now."

My head is spinning, trying to understand what the hell just happened.

"I've ruined everything."

"Shh." I rub her back as she cries. "It's going to be okay. Everything is going to be okay. You still have me. You have your family, your job, your friends. We will figure this out. Together. And then everything will be better."

"Danielle, you have to get out of bed today. I want you to come to work with me today. I think seeing the kids will do you a lot of good."

"No. I'm staying in bed."

"Honey, it's been a month. I know it's hard, but you can't stay in this bed forever. You have to get out and join the real world again."

"No."

"I'll take you to your favorite restaurant for lunch, and then tonight, we can drink wine and watch movies all night long. That will be fun, right?" I say, trying to use bribes to get her out of bed.

"No."

I frown, and then I get desperate. I grab her ankles and start pulling her out of bed. She fights me the whole time, grabbing hold of her headboard to stay in bed.

"God, you're freakishly strong."

"I'm not going anywhere. I'm not up for seeing people who know what I did."

"No one at my work knows what happened. They don't know you or your story. And the kids sure as hell don't. Just come with me. I could use a friend today."

"What do you need a friend for? You have a perfect life that could never fuck you over. Your perfect job with your perfect boyfriend and your perfect body and perfect money."

"Wes and I split up."

She sits up just a little. "Good. That will just make room for a more perfect boyfriend to come in and replace him."

"Come on, Danielle. I could really use a friend today. I need you."

She throws the covers over her head. "You have plenty of friends. I can't help you."

Two months later, Danielle finally made an appearance. She got out of bed, got dressed, and walked right out of the condo without even saying a word to me.

I couldn't help but smile from seeing her out of bed.

And then, two days later, the same. And then the next day and the next until she was getting out of bed more days than she was staying in it.

I thought she was doing better. I thought she'd finally decided one day that the men in her life were no longer the most important things. I thought she was choosing living.

I didn't realize that she was still depressed. And that, when she started leaving, it was actually the most dangerous part of her healing.

"Hey, Danielle. I need to borrow that pink lace shirt that you said didn't fit you anymore!" I yell through her bedroom door.

She doesn't answer.

I knock. "Danielle?"

She doesn't answer.

I smile when I look down at my watch. I'm running a bit late today. Danielle must have gone into work early. She works at a marketing company.

I push the door open to just grab the shirt I need myself. We are always borrowing each other's clothes and never care when the other borrows something without asking first.

I scream when I see her and then immediately gather my composure to run over to her. A needle is sticking out of her arm as she lies in her bed.

"Danielle," I say, gently tapping her face.

She doesn't move, but I do see her chest rise and fall. She's still breathing—for now.

"Come on, Danielle! Wake up!"

She moans softly as I tap her face harder, but she doesn't wake up. I grab my phone and dial 911. I don't know what else to do. The operator gives me some instructions to try and wake her up. But, most importantly, I just need to make sure she is still breathing when the paramedics arrive.

I hold her head in my lap as I wait.

"I'm so sorry, Danielle. I'm so, so sorry." I pat her hair.

She looks so peaceful, lying in my arms like this, but I know she is anything but at peace.

"I'm so sorry I didn't realize what was going on. I should have known after this happened before. I'm an idiot. Just please don't die, and I'll be here for you. I'll make this better. I promise."

I place my hand on Danielle's tombstone and then fold my legs as I take a seat in front of it.

"I'm so sorry I couldn't keep my promise. I couldn't save you. I thought I could. I thought that, once you healed and went to rehab, they would be able to help you. They couldn't. I thought our friendship would be enough to save you. It wasn't."

I let the tears fall down my face.

"I thought that a lot of love could save you, but it couldn't."

I cry for a long time, just sitting there with her. I don't know if I will ever get over her death. It was so senseless. It was all because a stranger came into her life and played games with her heart. The coroner's report said that she died because of an overdose. That's not true. She died from a broken heart that was never able to heal.

"Sloane?" I hear Wes behind me.

I stand up and wipe my tears.

"I was in town and thought I would come see how you were doing. Not well, huh?"

I shake my head.

"I'm so sorry about your friend."

"Thank you."

"I wish there were something I could do to help you. I could go kick that guy's ass if you want."

I smile and then cock my head to the side, looking at Wes. "Maybe there is something you can do to help me."

"What do you mean?"

"You can propose."

He frowns. "I care about you, Sloane, and I would do anything for you, but I don't think you and I getting married is going to fix anything. You and I don't work as a couple."

I shake my head. "I mean, to help me get revenge. Propose. Pretend we are getting married. Let the asshole steal me from you. And then I'll rip out his heart, like he did to Danielle."

"But, to do that, he would have to want to steal you."

"He will. I know how his game works. I'll just dangle myself in front of him, and then he'll try to steal me."

"But won't you hurt your family when you don't marry me?"

I shake my head. "The only person that is left to hurt is my grandmother. I'll tell her the truth."

He nods, still thinking. "This is a lot of work for something that might not work out the way you planned."

I nod. "I have to do it. For Danielle."

He nods, still thinking. "He has to fall in love with you to make this work."

"He will."

I look at Wes in the eyes, and I know he's still in love with me. Making men fall in love with me is never the problem. I always have the problem of falling in love with the man.

Wes nods, obviously agreeing that he will fall in love with me. "You can't fall in love with him."

I laugh. "I won't."

TWENTY-TWO

Asher

"I killed her," I say when Sloane finishes telling me her story.

Sloane nods solemnly.

"I knew I was a monster, but I never thought what I was doing was killing people."

I look at the tears that are now filling Sloane's eyes.

"I'm so sorry about Danielle. I never imagined that, that could happen. I'm so sorry she's gone. I'm so sorry that it was my fault. I'm so sorry I caused you so much pain."

"Sorry won't bring her back. That's the problem. I thought hurting you would make me feel better. Would get justice for what you did to Danielle. But nothing can change the only thing that would make any difference. Danielle is dead, and nothing will bring her back."

I feel my own tears welling in my eyes, looking at how much pain I've caused her. So much pain. And for what? So that I could play a game. So that I could have excitement in my life. It wasn't worth it.

"If I could take it all back, I would."

Sloane looks into my eyes, studying me for a moment. "I

believe you would, but you can't. And, every time I look at you, all I feel is pain."

I swallow a lump in my throat. She doesn't have to say anything more. I can already tell she means it, even when I thought she was in love with me, all she felt was pain, hurt, and anger. None of it was real. That is what she is trying to say. I'm just not sure I believe her. She has to be one hell of an actress to have slept with me. To have gotten me to fall in love with her and not feel anything in return.

"I thought I came here for closure. So that I could move on with my life and no longer be in pain. So that I might have a real chance at falling in love again," I say.

She raises an eyebrow when I say *love*.

"But I realize now, that's not why I came here. I didn't come back here so that I could erase the pain you caused me. I came back because I love you, and I want to feel that pain every day.

"Now that I did something so unforgivable, I think it's only right that I live with that pain every day. And I want you to be that reminder whether you are mine or not. I have to try to repay my debt to Danielle, to you, to the world.

"So, even though I know there is no chance of you ever loving me, I will always love you. There won't be other women in my life, only you. There won't be any more stealing, only giving. I can't ask for forgiveness. All I can do is love you with all of my heart and deal with the consequences from what I caused."

Sloane hasn't taken a breath the entire time I've been talking. She just looks at me, frozen.

"Breathe," I say.

She does, and then I continue, "The first time I stole was after my father died. He'd died in an armed robbery. The thieves got a hundred dollars in cash. A hundred dollars in cash. That is what my father died for. Something so incredibly ridiculous. I couldn't make sense of it. The first time I stole, it was electric. I felt a rush like I'd never felt before. I realized that was why the thieves had stolen. Not because they wanted the money or reward at the end. It was the thrill of doing something you weren't supposed to do, something that you might get caught doing.

"I know you can't understand why I would steal when my father died that way. I guess it was my way of dealing and coping. I didn't ever carry a gun or any weapon when I robbed. I just wanted to feel alive again."

"You might not believe me, but I understand why. My grandfather died of smoking, which only made me smoke more. Cigars, anything I could get my hands on. It just helps you feel closer to that person in some way. I get it," she says.

I nod. "But, once I started, I was addicted. I couldn't stop. I ended up in jail countless times. And then, when I realized I had to stop, I couldn't.

"But then I accidentally stole a woman who was engaged. I got her to fall for me. I saw the pain I caused her and her fiancé. I became addicted to something new. I became addicted to stealing women. I thought it was better than breaking the law. I thought I was saving these women from what was eventually going to happen later. They were going to get married and then live miserable lives that would eventually lead to divorce. I didn't think love was real. And, if it was, I wanted them to prove it to me. Prove that love existed by staying away from me. By getting rid of me. None of them did though. Not one. They all gave in eventually."

"Danielle and Wade would have eventually divorced. And who's to say that she wouldn't have gone down the same path at that point? Not that it should make you feel any better," Sloane says.

"Don't worry. It doesn't. I'm done meddling in other people's lives. I did something so unforgivable that I will be spending the rest of my life trying to make things right."

"I did something unforgivable, too," Sloane says in a whisper.

Her words make my heart stop. I suck in a breath.

She cheated on me. She lied to me about loving me. She set me up to hurt me in the same way that I hurt Danielle. She might have had a good reason for doing so, but what she did is still unforgivable. I can never look at Sloane again without seeing his hands on her naked body. I can never hear her moan my name again without thinking about his name escaping her lips.

We each did something unforgivable.

I look at her eyes, and my heart stops again. "You loved me. That part wasn't a lie, was it?"

She doesn't answer right away. But she slowly shakes her head. "It wasn't a lie," she whispers.

My eyes widen. I have no reason to trust this woman. She has every reason to hurt me again and again and again. And I have every reason to not trust a damn word out of her mouth. But I trust her because, if there is one thing that I know to be true, it is that we loved each other.

"You still love me?" I whisper.

TWENTY-THREE

Sloane

"Yes," I whisper back before biting my lip.

I hate myself for loving him. I shouldn't love him. He is the reason my friend is gone. Or, at least, a contributing factor. Although there are countless things I could blame for her death —Wade, drugs, Asher, Danielle, and myself—blaming anyone isn't going to bring her back.

What Danielle would have wanted, I hope, is for me to be happy. To keep living when she couldn't.

So, as crazy and stupid as it might be for me to love Asher, to trust that he has changed, I do. Because I love him.

"Can we try this again?" Asher asks, his little fingers brushing against mine in the sand.

I grin just a little. It's the first time I have in the weeks since I betrayed Asher. "Yes."

Our hands grasp each other's faces as we kiss. Our kisses are desperate, like we haven't seen each other in years, not weeks. Our tongues tangle together as well as our bodies in the sand.

As I kiss Asher, I realize how stupid I was for following through with my plan. I would have been walking down the same path that Danielle did instead of following my heart and finding happiness.

I feel the wind blow through us as we kiss. I shiver as it does. Asher wraps his arms around me tighter, kissing me, unable to stop.

The wind blows harder, and I get sand in my eye, causing me to stop kissing him for a second. When I get the sand out, he goes in for another kiss. I hold up my hand, stopping him. The look of pain on his face is so sad, it's almost cute.

"Are you having second thoughts?" he asks, his voice a little shaky.

I laugh because I love him so much that there is no way I could give him up, yet he still doubts how I feel. It's going to take him longer to heal than it will take me. But then I've had months to heal from his betrayal, and he's only had days to heal from mine.

"No. I just want to fuck you in a bed like normal people instead of here on the beach."

Asher laughs, and I immediately see his insecurity leave his face. He stands up and then motions for me to climb on his back. I do, and then he carries me while I kiss his neck on the way to his car.

We make it back to my condo building without completely stripping each other naked although it was hard to keep our hands off each other. At one point, I had to sit on my hands to keep Asher from crashing the car. He said he couldn't crash it. It wasn't even his car.

I'll have to ask him later where he has been sleeping since I took everything in the divorce. But I don't want to bring up negative things like that now. Right now, I want to remember one of the reasons that I fell in love so hard with Asher. Because of what he does to my body.

But we can't keep our hands off of each other any longer. Even though we still have to make it upstairs, into my condo, and then into bed.

Asher grabs my face and kisses me as soon as we are in the lobby. Sucking all of my breath away and making me wet with want and need for him.

"I can't wait to have you," I say between kisses.

"We need to move before they kick us out of the lobby," Asher says against my lips.

"Uh-huh," I say, tangling my hand in his hair that is starting to grow back out again.

Asher lifts me up, and I wrap my legs around his waist as he walks to the elevators.

"Miss Hart and Mr. Calder, it's so good to see you together again. I thought you might work it out," Archie says.

Asher sets me down while we wait for the elevator, but his hands stay on my waist as he kisses my cheek and neck, just giving my lips a break so that I can answer Archie.

"We are happy to be back together."

The elevator doors open, and Asher pushes me inside. "Thanks, Archie. We'll see you later."

The elevator doors close, and Asher pushes me against the wall as he kisses down my neck, then chest, and then stomach.

"Slow down, baby. We still have ten floors to climb."

Asher pumps his fist against the emergency button, and the elevator comes to a stop.

"What are you do—" I stop speaking or caring about what he is doing when he lifts my dress up and kisses my bare skin and then down the inside of my thigh.

"I know you want me to wait to fuck you until we get to your bed, but I can't wait to taste you. To make you mine again, especially after what he did to you."

I slip my panties down, and then he runs his tongue across my pussy.

"This is mine," he says against my skin.

I grab his hair as he licks over me, flicking his tongue across my clit, and then he slips a finger inside my pussy.

I bite my lip as he does it again and again, fucking me with his tongue, while I stand against the wall of the elevator. It's wrong and dirty and oh-so right.

He shows me exactly what he wants, what he needs, with his tongue. Me.

"I love this pussy," Asher says between licks. "Tell me you're mine. Tell me you want me. Tell me you need this," he says as he licks me faster.

I moan and feel myself getting close to exploding. I don't know how he expects me to say so much when he's doing what he is doing to me.

"Fuck, Asher," is all I can manage to get out.

I scream and come all over his face in the elevator that I'm sure Archie is frantically trying to fix.

Asher grins as he slowly stands up to see me breathing hard, my heart racing, and my cheeks flushed.

"I love you, Sloane."

"I love you, too. Although I think you need to do that at least a dozen more times before I start liking you again."

Asher laughs as he hits the button to start us moving again. He kisses me on the neck. "That can be arranged."

"See, I told you we would eventually make it to a bed," Asher says, holding me close, as I lie in my bed on his bare chest.

I grin. "All the other places are nice, but I still think I like the bed the best."

"Me, too. Although the ocean is a close second," he says, winking.

He runs his hand through my hair. "So, are you going to let me move in since you stole my house, my truck, and all my money?"

I wince. I was waiting for him to ask about it. "I kind of gave everything to the charity I run."

Asher laughs. "I knew you didn't like my shack."

I sit up and look at him. "I love your shack. It's the one thing I didn't sell or donate."

"I don't believe that you kept it."

"Of course I kept it. Besides, I don't think I would have been able to sell it. Nobody else would have wanted it, and if I had managed to sell it, I wouldn't have made money off of it anyway," I say.

Asher tickles me in retaliation. I giggle and squirm and swat at his hand to get him to stop.

When we both stop laughing, I say, "Can I move in with you though?"

Asher looks at me seriously. "You want to move into my place? You do know, I was telling the truth. That, that is my only place. You would have gotten any other place I had in the divorce if I'd had another place."

I nod. "I know. And maybe not right away. But, eventually, that is my hope. If you have taught me one thing, it is that I should live more simply. I live a life of giving back to others, yet I live in this place that has far too many things."

"I would love to have you share my shack with me as long as we bring this bed." Asher kisses me on the cheek. "This bed is far better than my bed."

I laugh. "We can bring the bed. When is your next competition?"

Asher frowns. "I have no idea. I haven't been training since you left me. Why?"

I grin and flip over, kissing his chest. "First, I want you to fuck me again and again in this bed."

Asher nods. "I'm listening."

"And then I want to talk about how you are going to work at my charity and continue surfing because you need to do both. You are great with the kids."

He kisses me on the cheek.

"And then we can talk about our future. When we are going to move in together, get married, have our own kids. Because, if there is one thing I know, it is that I love you, and I'm never hurting you again."

He kisses down to my breasts. "We can definitely talk about all of that. But I think we can wait to have the kids talk a little down the line." He takes my nipple in his mouth. "But I'm definitely up for practicing."

He grins.

"You did teach me the one thing you promised when you married me."

He thinks for a moment. "What was that again?"

"You taught me how to take risks. Because being with you is by far the riskiest thing I have ever done."

He grins. "Sometimes, taking the risk makes living worthwhile."

"And, sometimes, falling in love is all the adrenaline you need in your life."

He takes my nipple back in his mouth, ready for another round. One thought flashes through my head though, but I know I have only seconds left before the thought evaporates while Asher teases my body.

Should I tell him the truth?

No.

The truth isn't always needed to make a relationship work. Sometimes, a lie is needed to keep two people on even ground. Asher needs the lie to be true even if he suspects himself that it is false. He needs me to have done something unforgivable. Even though I didn't actually cheat on him with Chance, I did do something unforgivable. I lied.

I made Asher believe that I'd betrayed him. Cheated on him. I put images in his head that I know he will never be able to erase. But he needs to believe the lie. So, I will keep on lying about it. Just this once.

He stole to find love. I lied to keep it. But I have no doubts that our love will last because the one thing I don't have to worry about is that we will each do anything and everything to keep it.

EPILOGUE

Asher

Six Months Later

I've been patient. Trying to give her a normal relationship. Trying not to rush us, like our relationship was rushed in the past, but it has been the hardest goddamn thing I have ever done. Waiting. I hate waiting.

But it has been six months since she said she was willing to give us a second chance. Five months since she moved into my shack. Four months since we thought she was pregnant. Three months since I won my latest competition and actually started earning money again. Two months since we sold her condo. And one month since we found out we are expecting twins. Twins.

She doesn't want me to propose or for us to get married until after the babies are born, but I am not going to let that happen. I want the world to know that she is mine. That these babies are mine before they are born.

If it were up to me, we would have been married months ago. But I know she wanted to do things right this time. I'm not waiting nine months though until the babies are born. I'm proposing tonight, and then whether she likes it or not, we are getting married within the next couple of months.

"You're wearing that to go to dinner?" I ask, looking at Sloane sitting on the couch, wearing shorts and a tank top with her bikini straps sticking out of the top of her tank.

"Yes. You were the one who taught me to always be ready to go into the ocean. I'm not going to swim in my sundress, like what happened last time."

I frown, but she doesn't look up from her magazine that she is flipping through. I don't know how I'm going to get her into a dress. I don't think the restaurant I'm taking her to would approve of shorts.

"But I love you in that pink dress you wear. You could wear your bikini under it, and that way, I could do dirty stuff to you while we are seated at the table."

Sloane sighs. "Fine, you win. I'll change." She gets up from the couch and walks over to the small closet she made in the corner. She pulls out the dress, starts to undress, and then puts it on.

"Thank you," I say, kissing her on the cheek. Sloane picks up her magazine again.

"Look at these cribs. They are made for twins, but they're smaller. It would be perfect over in this corner," she says.

My eyes pop open. "We are not living here once the babies are born. We don't have enough space! They need their own rooms. Babies come with stuff. Lots and lots of stuff. We need to start looking for a new place. I would have said your condo would work, but of course, we sold that. But maybe this is the perfect opportunity. We could get a four- or five-bedroom house with a nice yard."

Sloane laughs. "Five bedrooms? We don't have any family that visits us. Why do we need five bedrooms?"

"When we have more kids."

She laughs again. "I think the two on the way are more than enough for now. And we don't need to move. We have plenty of space for them here."

I rub the back of my neck and take a deep breath. I will argue with her about getting a new place later. For now, I just want this night to go perfectly.

I glance at my watch. "You ready?"

She nods and smiles. I hold out my arm, and she takes it with a raised eyebrow, not used to me being so gentlemanly. She glances at my attire for the first time. I'm not wearing a suit. I figured that would be a little too obvious, but I am wearing khakis and a button-down shirt.

"You look nice," she says.

"And you look beautiful, as always." I chastely kiss her on the lips. I don't want us to get too carried away, like we have in the past, and not make it out of here.

I lead her out of the shack, and she stops in shock when she sees the limo I arranged for.

"Why are we going somewhere in a limo?"

I grin. "Because we have been dating for six months, and I want to celebrate without worrying about getting arrested for driving a nice car. Plus, we can do dirty things on the way back."

"Not on the way there?"

"No. I want to make sure my girls are well fed."

I lead her to the limo, and we climb in.

"What makes you think the twins are girls?" she asks.

"Because the universe knows better than to make another of anything remotely like me. If they are girls, then they will take after you, not me."

She laughs. "Well, I think, whatever they are, if they take a little after you, it won't be that bad."

I hold her hand as we drive to the restaurant I picked out. My hands are so sweaty though that I'm sure she has already figured out what is going on. I'm surprised she hasn't said anything about me not proposing tonight. So, at least, I'm happy with that.

We get to the restaurant, and I help Sloane out of the car. I hold her hand while we walk into the restaurant.

"Do you have a reservation, sir?"

"Yes, under Asher Calder."

"Just one moment, and I'll take you to your table."

"Hey, guys. What are you doing here?" Luca asks as he walks out of the bar area of the restaurant.

"Hey, Luca," Sloane says, giving him a hug. "Having dinner. Want to join us?"

I eye Luca, trying to let him know that he is not to have dinner with us.

"I'd love to. This place has great food. It's on me. I've heard that congratulations are in order," Luca says.

I grimace at Luca. He does not take a hint.

"You told him," Sloane says to me with a frown on her face, thinking that I told him about the twins.

I haven't.

"No. Luca likes to lie and joke a lot. Like I've told you before, you can never trust a word out of Luca's mouth."

Sloane ignores me though. "I can't believe you told him we are pregnant with twins."

"You're pregnant with twins! That's amazing! Good job, buddy," Luca says, slapping me on the back.

I glare at him, trying to make him stop, but there is no use.

"Wait...what were you congratulating us on if you didn't know about the twins?" Sloane asks.

"Your engagement, of course. All I've heard for the last month is, should he or shouldn't he use the same ring that he bought for you when he was going to propose last time? So, which did you go with?" Luca says.

Sloane turns to me. "Last time?"

I can see her wheels turning, and there is no use in making sure everything is proper and right. Not anymore.

I take Sloane's hand. I get down on one knee, and I pull the box out of my pocket.

"Sloane, I wanted tonight to go perfectly. I wanted to show you how much I love you with all the romance you deserve. But, as usual, that is not how things go with us. But I can't go one more day, minute, second without telling you that I love you more than anything. And I'm beyond excited to spend the rest of our lives together. Will you please, please marry me? I know I don't deserve it. But I promise to spend the rest of my life making it up to you."

She grins. "Yes."

I put the ring that I chose the first time on her finger and then stand up and kiss her, no longer caring if we have dinner or not. I can't contain my excitement.

"Good choice. I told you she would want the original ring that you were going to propose with until you found out that she was cheating on you," Luca says, staring down at the ring that is in the shape of a wave on her finger.

"Get out of here," I say to him between kisses.

"What? You don't want your best friend here to celebrate with you?" he asks.

"No, Luca," Sloane and I say at the same time.

"Fine, fine. I wouldn't want to hang out with thieves like you anyway," Luca says as he walks back to the bar.

I grin. "I wouldn't want to hang out with a liar like you either."

He smiles and waves. Then, he leaves Sloane and me to celebrate.

"So, what are you hungry for, future Mrs. Calder?"

"You. And, just so you know, I'm keeping my name."

I sigh. "As long as I get to call you my wife, I don't care." I stare at Sloane as she looks down at her ring and then back up at me. Her whole body is glowing with excitement. But even through the excitement I know that she is hiding something from me. And I know exactly what that secret is. I cornered Chance, the bastard lawyer that was in her bed. It was easy to persuade him to tell me the truth. I can seem pretty intimidating when I'm angry and threaten to cause him pain.

She never slept with him. She just paid him to pretend that they were cheating. And the look in her eyes now confirms his story.

I won't tell her that I know her secret. It's a lie I bet she plans on taking to her grave. It may not be as bad as ruining someone's life like I did, but it is still a lie. I stole her heart, she lied to claim mine. All that matters is that we love each other.

Free Books

Want to read along for **free** as I write a new novel—*Not Sorry*?

Want to get my **free** bonus novella—***Aligned: Ever After?***

Want to know when I put my books on sale for **free or 99 cents**?

You can get all of the above and more goodies here:
EllaMiles.com/freebooks

More Books

BY ELLA

Heart of a Liar is the next book in the Unforgivable Romance series and features Luca and Ivy.

Pre-Order Here

Other Books by Ella:

Too Much

Aligned Series

Maybe Series

Definitely Series

About Ella

Ella Miles writes steamy romance with a twist. She's currently living her own happily ever after near the Rocky Mountains with her high school sweetheart husband. Her heart is also taken by her goofy four year old black lab that is scared of everything, including her own shadow.

Ella is the author of the Amazon bestselling book: TOO MUCH. She is also the author of the ALIGNED series, MAYBE series, and DEFINITELY series. Get a free book by visiting her website: EllaMiles.com/freebooks.

Stalk me at:
www.EllaMiles.com
ella@ellamiles.com

Acknowledgments

This book was really fun to write and practically wrote itself. I love writing characters that are completely broken, messed up, and make all the wrong choices in life. Who wants a perfect book boyfriend anyway? I hope that you have found that you can still fall in love with a book boyfriend that is a little less than perfect. Because Asher and the rest of the characters that you will meet in the rest of the Unforgivable Series are all far from perfect. But they all have a love story to tell and I can't wait for you to read about them!

Of course, I have too many people to thank and will probably forget some. But I must thank my editor, Jovana, and my proofreader, Jenn. Thank you for cleaning up my words to make my story as perfect as it can be.

Thank you Cara for making me an awesome cover that fits this book so well. This was our first "Fabio" cover that we did for any of my books, meaning the first cover that just has a shirtless man with lots of nice abs and I'm sure it won't be the last ;)

Thank you to my street team for reviewing and helping me to promote the book as always! You guys are my truest fans and I can't believe I'm so lucky to have found so many amazing friends and fans along this journey so far.

Thank you to my awesome husband who helped with almost every step including: editing, proofreading, formatting, and tech support. He's the best!

Last but not least, thank you to you, my reader! Thank you for taking the time out of your busy life to read my book! For taking a chance on a book that maybe isn't your typical romance. For reading about a couple that I'm sure made you angry and frustrated as you read, but still fell in love with both of them despite their flaws. Thank you for reading!

If you enjoyed the book, please consider leaving a review. I can't thank you enough if you do!! :)